Albany De Fonblanque

Pious Frauds

A novel

Albany De Fonblanque

Pious Frauds
A novel

ISBN/EAN: 9783337029418

Printed in Europe, USA, Canada, Australia, Japan

Cover: Foto ©Andreas Hilbeck / pixelio.de

More available books at **www.hansebooks.com**

A Novel

BY

ALBANY DE FONBLANQUE

AUTHOR OF "A TANGLED SKEIN," "FILTHY LUCRE," "BAD LUCK,"
"CUT ADRIFT," ETC.

IN THREE VOLUMES

VOL. III

LONDON

RICHARD BENTLEY AND SON

Publishers in Ordinary to Her Majesty the Queen

1880

CONTENTS OF VOL. III.

PIOUS FRAUDS.

CHAPTER I.

THE LAND-SLIP.

WHEN the little antiquary was quite out of sight, Cowper drew forth the packet already described, and talked to it as though it could hear him. "If I take you home and burn you, I shall have to open you, and then some of those old temptations—d—— them! may come to life again. That won't do. I'll dispose of you here; and now I'll take a hint from that poor fool, Poynder, and send you with a boulder round your neck to the bottom of his hole; there to

III. 40

remain till the crack of doom. That's the
way. Sib is provided for and happy, with
more than she ever hoped for. The boy,
poor lad! is not fit to be a Bellmonte. I
doubt if he'll live to be a man, and if he
does, why Arthur will take care of him if I
can't. I can tell him *some* of the truth.
And I can put it out of my power ever to
tell it all. If I were to do as Poynder did
no one—yes, they would. They'll come
raking after my body and find the papers.
That won't do. George Cowper must live,
but Sir George Bellmonte—by jingo it *is* a
suicide, now I think of it; only no one will
be missed."

He skirted the foot of the hill, and made
for a place up stream where there was a
shallow — silver-sand and gravel — through

which a little back-water from Poynder's hole used to trickle. He was surprised to find this running deep and strong. Here were plenty of stones. To reach them he had to scramble down the bank, which was some ten feet high, and did so, aided by the roots of an ancient pollard willow which stood, thick and stumpy, on the top. " Another such flood as we had last year, my friend," he said to the tree, " and down you'll come." Then he began searching for stones, musing half aloud as he went: " There must be no slipping, so these round fellows won't do. Ah ! you look more likely ; so here goes." He straightened out the piece of line he had begged of Moule, wet it so that the knots should not slip, laid the stone he had chosen on his knee, placed the packet on it, and began to lash the two together. Standing up, the operation was not easy, and there was no place to sit and perform it with the exactitude it required. " I'll go back to the hole," he said, " and—"

As he thus resolved, a low crackling noise startled him. Instinctively he thrust the package back into his breast, and made for the bank. He looked up and saw that the crest of Castle Hill was scored with a great yellow gash. He saw the whole green river side of it give a heave and a shiver, and then—with a roar louder than the loudest thunder—it crashed downwards, carrying all before it into the *Gar!* The next instant he was himself dashed to the earth.

*   *   *   *

He was found half-buried by the fallen

bank, with the tree he had foredoomed
prostrate on his chest.   He had escaped the
main rush of the land-slip—better for him,
perhaps, if he had not.   His right arm was
broken, his left doubled under him; a thin
line of blood trickled from his mouth.   On
each side of where he was the bank had
given way entirely; the portion immediately
over his head was held up from overwhelm-
ing him only by the upturned roots of the
fallen tree; and the tree was crushing him
to death ! The river, completely dammed by
the land-slip, was rising fast, so three modes
of death awaited him.   In less than half-an-
hour of the catastrophe two hundred people
were crowded around the spot, and not one
could help him, save by clearing away the
sand that flowed down from above upon his

face, and complying with his constant moan for water. At last Doctor Barwell arrived, and began to storm about nothing having been done. It was explained to him that if the tree were raised, the bank would fall. "Well, then, prop up the tree," came out of his clear head, "and dig him out from underneath." So they cut wedge-like logs and drove them under the trunk of the pollard willow, so that its weight rested on them, and thus relieved Cowper spoke for the first time. "Send for Moule," he whispered, "quick! Let no one touch me but Moule."

"Your wife is here," said Doctor Barwell. "Steady there, my men, you're hurting him." But it was no bodily hurt which brought that sudden gasp from the crushed and dying man.

"Tell—her—to—go—home," he faltered; "this is no place for women. Oh, Milly— you—must—not—stop—"

Hearing that he had spoken, she came through the press and stood, pale but tearless, by his side.

"Humour him," whispered the Doctor in her ear, "see how excited he is!"—and so she retired.

"Will—Moule—ne—ver come!"

A dozen messengers had been sent for him, but he could not be found. The fact was, that on his way home he had turned out of the high-road to where a well was being sunk. Now it often happened that well-sinkers come upon what seem to them a lot of "broken pots and things," but which to our antiquary were priceless specimens of

old ceramic art. So he stood by like a
venerable terrier in spectacles at a rat-hole,
watching the buckets as they came up, and
when at last he started homeward again, and
was found on the main road, it was quite
night.

In the mean time relays of strong and
willing hands carried out Doctor Barwell's
orders. It was easy to say, "Dig him out
from underneath," but the light, dry, sandy
soil fell in almost as fast as they shovelled it
out, and all knew that the end was at hand.
They might dig out the body. Death was
working quicker than their spades.

"Doctor," murmured the dying man, so
low that Barwell had to kneel over him and
place his ear to his mouth to hear, " is Moule
—here—yet?"

" Not yet."

" How long shall I live ? "

" Wait till they get you out, and then I can say where you are hurt," replied the doctor.

" I—am—hurt—all—over ; my—breast— bone—is—crushed—in—"

" Never mind ; people have lived with worse than that."

" I—am—dying—Doctor. Is—the—Castle —Hill—all—gone ? "

" Every bit of it."

" Where—was—the—slip ?—below the path —or—"

" Above it, on the very crest."

" Then," said his questioner—and his pallid face lit up with a gleam of triumph—" the Sinking Stones are gone."

"Gone into the *Gar*, and buried there—thank God," replied Barwell; "they'll drive no more Bellmontes crazy. Now don't waste the little strength you have talking."

But Cowper doesn't hear, or hearing heed.

"You—don't—believe—the—legend?"

"Who does?"

"Stick to that—Doctor; it's a foolish—old—lie. Sir Arthur—isn't—hurt—and—Doctor, tell him that I have been true to him, but—that—Fate—was—too much for me. Tell him that if I had been used to pray—oh, God!"

Every care had been taken to prop up the tree, but the excavation made beneath it, or perhaps the rising of the river, caused the earth to slip. It slid only about a foot, but that was enough. He died with the name of his Maker on his lips, and his last thought was loyal to the race he loved.

* * * *

It was now a contest in the dark with the rapidly-rising water, to lift the fallen tree, or have it floated off. More help had come now —when it was too late—with horses and ropes, and they raised it easily. The body was carried up to the bank, where a hurdle was ready to take it to what had been its home. At this moment, his poor distracted old friend staggered through the crowd, and flung himself upon his knees beside the corpse.

"George, George!" he cried—"no, not dead—he cannot be dead. The Lord have mercy upon us!—the whole hill is down. George! you sent for me. I'm here. Stand back, good people, pray. I know he has something of the greatest importance to tell me."

"Mr. Moule," said the widow, stepping forward, and laying a hand on his arm. "I will allow no interference with my husband's body."

"He sent for me—he wished—" pleaded the antiquary, breathless with haste and grief—"I was his friend."

"I was his wife, sir; I have the best right to order here. I wish my husband's body to be taken, just as it is, to my house."

"And I protest against anything of the kind," cried the antiquary, jumping up and facing her. "Dr. Barwell, you are the coroner, and your voice, I fancy, is the one that is to prevail in this matter."

" Not against the feelings of relations, Mr. Moule."

" Feelings! Don't you know better than that, Doctor? My poor dear friend swore he never would enter that—that lady's house. Right or wrong, with reason or without, does not matter now. He swore he wouldn't, and all that Sir Arthur could say, and I could say, did not move him from his determination. Why, it was only yesterday that I got upon the subject again, and he was as positive as ever. I say that his feelings should be respected, though he is dead."

" And I, that death has silenced resentment," replied Mrs. Cowper, coolly, not to Moule (whom she affected to ignore), but to Dr. Barwell. " Will you be good enough to order that my wishes shall be obeyed? I myself will prepare the body for any examination that has to be made. I will provide the funeral. I desire that my husband's corpse be taken exactly as it is to my house."

"A distance of over three miles," pleaded Moule, "when his own cottage isn't one."

"I really do think, Mrs. Cowper," Dr. Barwell observed, "that it would be more convenient—"

"I am really surprised you should be so thoughtless," retorted the widow angrily; "convenient! Is that the word to use against the demand—yes, sir, the demand of a wife. Convenient indeed! Have you thought for a moment what is to follow if this *convenient* course is adopted? Who is to lay out the body?—his housekeeper? Well, I can tell you that she has run off into the town half dead with fright, and would not come out here again for a hundred pounds."

"Then I'll do it myself," Moule cried in desperation. "I'll answer for everything."

"Then," she continued, not noticing the interruption, "you save two miles now, how many is it going to cost you before it's all over?"

Dr. Barwell thinks of that long tramp for the jury, for the surgeon who is to make the autopsy, for those who will have to attend the funeral; and his ideas of *convenience* chop right round.

"She's right, Moule," he decided; "it's no use talking. She was his wife, and has a right to her own way in this. Think it over in the morning when you are more

calm, and you'll acknowledge it's so.   Why,
man (taking him on one side and whispering),
what in God's name makes you so excited
about it! The woman must have some
tender spot about her, or she wouldn't be
here."

"How long was she here before I
arrived?" asked Moule.

" I don't know; but what does it
matter?"

It mattered everything, but he dared
not say so. Had she already got possession of the packet? That was what
mattered.

" To please you, I'll ask," said Barwell,
who noticed the other's misery, and was
vexed at having to oppose a man he
respected.

" Oh, she was here first of all," replied the new head-keeper, when the question was put. " I met her running towards my house, when I started out to see what had happened."

" How long was that after the slip ? "

" About a quarter of an hour."

" What did she say ? "

" Come quick ; my husband is buried in the slide, or something like that. I don't exactly remember the words."

" Then they must have been together," cried Moule aghast.

" We were not," Mrs. Cowper replied ; " I happened to be in the neighbourhood, and I saw him on the bank, fishing as I suppose, just before the catastrophe. I cannot think why time should be wasted over these frivolous questions."

"He did not go straight home then," Moule thought, and a hope rose—that he had hidden or sunk the packet.

They covered the hurdle with ferns, placed what was once George Cowper upon it, and carried the body to the house he had sworn never to enter again. And there they left it. Having straightened the distorted limbs, closed the eyes, and drawn a sheet over all, Doctor Barwell departed, saying, "I will come back in an hour or two, Mrs. Cowper. Being Coroner, I cannot myself make the autopsy; I must fetch Goodlake. If I were you I wouldn't stay here; you can do nothing yet."

She went with him to the other room, and saw him depart. As soon as he had driven away, she went back, drew aside the sheet, and felt the poor mangled chest. "I thought so," she said; and her eyes flashed with joy as she drew forth the packet.

CHAPTER II.

"THE SADDEST OF LOVE, IS LOVE GROWN COLD."

WHEN we first had the honour of making the acquaintance of Mr. Norman Drummond, he was fairly successful at the bar for a man of his standing—that is to say, he paid the rent of his chambers, and part of the expenses of circuit and sessions out of his fees. The Bellmonte business came in when he married, and this put his practice into a ticklish position. At such a point a practice is very like a bad cold. It may go away, or it may turn to something serious. He

might be floated on to a silk gown and the
bench, or he might miss the turn, and drag
on into a greyheaded leader of sessions for
whom a chance would never come again.
He worked hard, and he worked luckily,
and before the time of George Cowper's
death he had that slippery thing — " a
reputation "—firmly in his grasp.

Nor was he alone in Fortune's smile. The
steady, sturdy work of his father had at last
made its mark, and caused his promotion to
a Deanery, which, if clerical gossip was to be
believed, would only be the stepping-stone
to a bishopric soon to be vacant.

Under such circumstances most men, I
think, would be more than content. A
beautiful and affectionate wife, a happy
home, the healthy tonic of success in the

present, and a glimpse of grateful ambition
in the future. But there are some minds in
which discontent requires gold to be gilt,
and Drummond's was one of them. It
began to dawn upon him that he had made
a mistake on that great subject of mistakes
—marriage. He thought he had gone much
too cheaply. If you imagine he loved Sib,
as such a woman desired to be loved, I have
failed in my attempt to delineate his character. He pursued her first to spite Arthur
Bellmonte, then to amuse himself, and then
because he was piqued at her indifference.
He married her because the lowest form of
passion blinded him; for some moments he
had held her splendid form clasped to his
heart. Love had little part in the emotions
which sprung out of such doings. And yet

he thought he loved her. When she was his wife, he would have sworn he loved her, and secretly was proud of himself for what he deemed to be an unselfish affection. I have noted that selfish people are often exceedingly fond of themselves, when they imagine they have done an unselfish act.

But this wore off. Sib was as beautiful as ever, loved him better than ever; but his old self-love returned, and whispered that she was a drag on him; that he could have done much better—very much better.

The legitimate demands of his profession caused him to leave her too much alone. Three circuits, and sessions eight times a year, do not leave the best of barrister spouses much time at home. And even when he was not on the (legal) tramp there was work to do at night which must be got through in chambers, where the books were kept, and perfect quiet reigned. Chelsea was such a long way from the Temple, that Norman Drummond had a bed put up in his chambers to use when he was detained very late at night, and had to be in Court early in the morning. At first he used it sparingly, but the time came when Sib did not see him for days together.

Could he not give up something, and not work so hard? pleaded Sib. He was injuring his health — not a sigh over her own loveliness.

"My dear, you don't understand these things," he replied, testily. "A man in my position must take all, or lose all." And he spoke the truth. Newspaper moralists gird

at lawyers for accepting more business than
they can do, but the public pick out their
favourites, and pile briefs upon them, knowing they cannot do justice to them all, but
each hoping that *his* case will be the lucky
one attended to.

There were social requisitions also which
could not be denied. He had to dine with
A because he was a judge, and it is well
to keep on good terms with the bench.
He had to dine with B because he led the
circuit, and was good-natured about refer-
ences. He had to dine with C because he
was an attorney. He had to dine with D
—" well, hang it! a man who worked as
hard as he did deserved some relaxation!"—
D was an old college chum he had not seen
for years, and had got up a little party at

Greenwich expressly in his (Mr. Drummond's) honour. For a long time it never
occurred to Sib to ask herself why Lady A
and the Madames B and C did not call on
her, and so enable her husband to return
their hospitality at home. When clients
came up from the country they dined with
him at his club—to save her trouble, he
said. She would not care about knowing
that sort of people.

The fact was that scarcely any of his
friends knew he was a married man. At
first he had no ambition of keeping the
main fact a secret, but was shy of provoking
questions as to the when and where of his
marriage. He thought he would wait a
while, and then he could say, "Oh! didn't
you know? It's an old story; I've been

married a long time." I wonder why it is
that when we hear of something we did not
know, and are told it took place long ago,
we lose interest in it, and ask no questions ;
but if it happened yesterday we want to
know all about it ? As time went on, Mr.
Norman Drummond not only refrained from
volunteering information about his marriage,
but he actually concealed and denied it. A
sneaking devil, whose utterances made him
despise himself for having such a counsellor,
whispered in his ear that perhaps after all
he was not married. He began by thinking
how much better off he would have been
if he were not. A pale face at home re-
proached him—not from its lips—he would
rather prefer her finding fault. Then he
could answer her. Many bright faces abroad

attracted him. If it were not for his wife,
he could accept the invitation of an ex-
tremely fashionable and dandy Q.C. to
accompany him abroad during the long
vacation to Paris, Baden-Baden, Trouville,—
all sorts of delightful places, where the Q.C.
aforesaid changed his raiment four times a
day, and was the darling of grand dames
and *les petites*, alike. He had a great mind
to go anyhow, for it would do him good to
be seen out in the fashionable world with
that Q.C. as his Mentor. And go he did.

What would the Bellmontes think!
That! for the Bellmontes. He began to
hate them as the fabricants of the mill-stone
he had hung round his neck. If it had not
been for Arthur he would never have undertaken that disastrous journey to Scotland.

And as for May—confound her! it was she
who persuaded her cousin into that "miserable jumping over a broomstick"—for such
the whispering devil called his marriage,
without rebuke.

Gratitude! What had the Bellmontes
done for him? Given him a wife he didn't
want; saddled him with an expensive house;
sent him business they must have paid *some*
one to do—and he had done it well. He had
made that bumptious Railway Company eat
humble-pie, and as for the dredging business
on the *Gar*, that was broken up by the land-
slip. He could do very well—now; without
the Bellmontes.

His going abroad with the dandy Q.C.
hurt Sib deeply. She had been so lonely,
so patient! Surely he might have taken

her! Her heart was sore at the loss of May, and rebelled against this unkindness and neglect—rebelled, and began to teach her truths which affection had hidden up to now.

"I see by to-day's paper," she said shortly after his return, "that your father is to preach in Westminster Abbey on Sunday. We must go and hear him. Of course you have asked him to stay with us?"

"I have not," her husband replied; "I believe he has come on a visit to the Dean."

"What day will suit you for me to ask him to dine?"

"Oh, he has heaps of engagements. He wouldn't care to dine with us."

"Not to see me? Surely, Norman, he takes sufficient interest in you to want to make the acquaintance of your wife."

"Well, to tell you the truth, he doesn't know I'm married."

"Not—know—you—are—married!" she cried aghast.

"Don't look so absurdly frightened, Sib. My father has left me pretty much to myself since I was eighteen. There was no occasion for me to ask leave and—and I put it off. You see he suffered himself from an early marriage when he was poor, and what was the good of making him anxious about me? I'll tell him some day."

"Some day will not do, Norman," Sib replied, still pale, and trembling with an unknown fear. "You are making a good income now, so according to your own notions you can tell him at once. I cannot say how surprised and pained I am that he

was not allowed to know it from the first.
Just imagine how vexed he would be, and
justly, if he learned it from some stranger.
A nice opinion he would have of me! He
would condemn us both, but *me* especially.
He would think I wanted to wean you away
from your family—accuse me of disrespect.
He would never love me. You must go
and see him on Sunday; promise me that
you will?"

"This is my affair, Sib, and I'm going to
manage it in my own way," he replied, getting angry; the first refuge for a man who
knows he is in the wrong. "It's by no
means as easy an affair to manage as you
suppose. I'll see him, of course, and feel
my way."

"Feel your way," she echoed him. "I

don't understand you. Feel your way to what? You have been independent of him since you were eighteen, you say. You are more than independent now. You have simply to tell him that you have a wife, and bring him to see her."

" Yes; and run the gauntlet of questioning about when we married, and where, and how?"

" Why not? He has a right to know."

" It will be very much better for me to wait till he goes back home and then write to him. I can then tell him just as much as I please, in writing; and if he asks questions in reply, answer or not as may be convenient. It's easy enough to slur things in a letter. If we were face to face, and I refused to satisfy him it would be very different."

" But, Norman, what should you refuse to satisfy him about—Uncle Tyrell? Surely, surely when Sir Arthur Bellmonte has married May, you—"

"That's not it"—he knit his brows, and his face grew dark and sullen. That whispering devil had him under the shadow of its wings, and was urging, " Have it out now —once for all; " but he was a moral coward, and dared not.

"Norman," she said, laying her hand on his arm, " cannot you trust me in this? If it is not Uncle Tyrell, what can it be? I have a right to know. Oh, Norman, for a man to keep his marriage secret does not matter much, perhaps; but for a woman!

It is terrible. Suppose your father were to speak of you as a single man to any one who knows us, what might they not think of me! Dear Norman, marriage is such a solemn, such a holy tie; it ought not to be trifled with."

He drew a long breath, as one who is about to lift a heavy weight. "My father," he said, speaking with deliberation, but not daring to look her in the face, "would agree with you in that. I did not want to tell you where the hitch is, but if you *must* know my father is a high churchman; very high, in some points—marriage, for example. He is one of those who condemn the idea that it is a civil contract, from which either party can, under any circumstances, withdraw by civil process. He takes the words, 'Whom

God has joined, let no man put asunder,'
literally."

"I think he is right," said Sib; "don't
you?"

"That is as it may be. But he
founds his objection on the fact of a
joining by God; that is, by a religious
ceremony, performed by an ordained
minister, in a church. I have to tell
you plainly, Sib, that he would utterly
disapprove of the manner in which you
became my—in which we acted in Scotland."

As he spoke, she rose, and stood before
him, white as a statue of Suspense, and
(outwardly) as cold.

"You were going to say in which you
became my wife; why did you hesitate,

and change your words? Am I your wife, Norman Drummond?"

"Tush! we were speaking of my father's prejudices—call them that, if you like."

"This is trifling with me, and with the truth. Your father's opinions on such a subject cannot be discussed as prejudices. If he holds to what you say it is a sacred conviction with such a man as he, and we should respect it. You must marry me again, as he would have us married."

"A pretty admission that would make!" he said, with a sneer. "You want to foul your own nest, do you? Marry you again, indeed! If another ceremony be necessary, how are you to account for living here all these months?"

"Oh, God! help me!" she cried, throwing up her hands to her all but bursting brows.

"You never think of a great many things," he replied, with an attempt at reproach, "and won't let me think for you; but you brought it on yourself. Why could not you leave me to deal with my father as I thought best?"

"Norman, are you sure, quite sure, that our marriage was a good one?"

"Lots of people think Scotch marriages good enough," he told her carelessly.

"It is not what *people* think. I want to know, and I must know, what *is*. Is what we did enough to make me, legally, your wife?"

"Yes; in Scotland."

"And we were in Scotland?" she mused,

some sense of relief coming to her rescue.

"*I suppose so*," he replied,* as though it were a question put to him ; "but we were very near the border. The road in front of the house where we stayed after the accident is the boundary, I hear. Now, I must really go to chambers, as I have a heavy brief to read. I shall not be back to-night."

And so he left her.

He was surprised to get off so easily, and hurried down the stairs so as to escape the scene he dreaded. He did not hear a dull, heavy thud on the floor above him, as he hastily took hat and

* This incident was composed, and partly written, in the month of July, 1876.

coat from the rack. "I'll leave that to soak," he said to himself, as he gained the street.

CHAPTER III.

" BECAUSE I LOVED YOU."

" HAVE you answered Tyrell's letter ?" asked Sir Arthur one day, when the Prices had departed, and our pair were left alone in Paris.

" Yes, dear ! I have."

" And if I may venture to ask, how much did you send him ? "

" Not a penny."

Arthur made no reply for a moment or two. What his wife did with her money was, he felt, her business. She had renounced a handsome settlement—surely she might use the comparatively small sum that was her own as she pleased.

" Do you think I ought to have given him what he wanted ?" asked May.

" Well, dear, since you put the question, I do think it would have been wise, from a selfish point of view. The more he rises, the better it will be for us. Besides getting into Parliament is a wonderful sedative for unruly spirits like Tyrell. They roar there like any sucking-doves."

" I thought people could not buy a seat in Parliament, now ? "

" Nor can they ; but there are heavy expenses about a canvass, and election."

" Uncle Tom used to rave at people who spent money on canvassing and elections."

" So do they all until they ruin themselves. It is not too late now. If I were you I'd send him the money."

" I'd rather not," said May; "I don't like the tone of his letter, Arthur; there's a flavour of black-mailing about it which puts my back up."

"Well, he's your uncle, not mine." Arthur was a little vexed at the rejection of his advice. "If you did make a promise to help him, his reminding you of it is natural enough; and one thing I must say, dear, I don't half like to see you getting so fond of hoarding money. What is it for? You don't spend it on yourself."

" You do not give me a chance, dear. You are extravagant enough upon me for both of us," she replied, laughing.

"Do you want to build a church, or

schools, or something like that when we get home ?"

" You'll see, in time."

" Because if that's what you are after, I don't mind. What I hate is, to think that my May, who used to be so generous with her small means, should look as though she were mean, now she is comparatively rich."

"Husband—darling !" cried his wife, with a sob, throwing her arms around his neck ; " do trust me, and—and be patient." He kissed her, and the subject dropped.

They had now been away three months ; and of course had received full and detailed accounts of the landslip, in which George Cowper had lost his life. May had written a letter of condolence to Mrs. Cowper, to which no reply came ; and Sir Arthur had ordered that the funeral should be conducted at his expense ; for which he got no thanks. This was greatly accounted for by a line in one of Lady Bellmonte's letters, in which she wrote that Mrs. Cowper had shut up her cottage, and left for parts unknown. "Is it not almost time," her ladyship continued, "for you runaways to come home ? Are you not tired of your own company yet ?"

It did not look like it as they sat side by side, reading this question with their arms round each other.

"Are we ?" asked May, looking up into his face.

"Are you ?"

"Not yet—are you ?"

Pair of fools !

They wrote to say they would be back by the end of November—certainly long before Christmas. They were going to Brussels, and should return by Antwerp.

Those were their plans. What could derange them? They were well, happy, liked travelling, and their time was their own. However, something did derange those plans. One morning the courteous gentleman in the Rue Castiglione who received their letters, and cashed Sir Arthur's cheques, gave him a business-like looking epistle, post-marked *Garcin*, which made him change colour. Fortunately May was not with him. He turned into the Tuilleries Garden, and sunk on a chair, his face turned up at the sky with a look of blank misery. So he remained for one hour before he summoned up courage to go to the hotel and meet his bride.

"Darling," he said, "I think we shall have to go home sooner than we arranged. Do you mind our holiday being cut short?"

"Not a bit; on the contrary, I'm glad. I want to see dear old Sib. I've been thinking over her last two letters, and I'm sure she's unhappy. Arthur, if Norman should prove a bad husband, I never would forgive myself. Fancy his going abroad and leaving her already!"

"Perhaps he had to do so. But we are wandering from the point. Could you get ready so as to start to-morrow?"

"There's something wrong," she answered, with a start. "Tell me what it is, Arthur— tell me all!"

"It is nothing that you could understand, dearie. Ucross wánts me for some
law business."

"About the landslip?"

"Yes," he replied quickly. "It dammed
up the river, and the millers—"

"Is that all! Give me two hours,"
laughed May, "and we shall both be
ready."

They started that night.

"Why, good Lord! Sir Arthur!" exclaimed the station-master at Bellmonte
junction—"the idea of you coming home
like this, and her ladyship too! without
anybody to welcome you! Why, it was
only last week that we were a-plotting
and a-planning what we would do to
celebrate your return, and here you are

right on us before we know where we
are ! "

" We thank you all the same, Mr. Badger,"
said he. "You've had trouble enough
about us already. I'm glad you have not
prepared a formal welcome, and please don't
let there be any."

When he went off duty that night, Mr.
Badger told Mrs. Badger that she could not
think how solemn they (the Bellmontes)
were. He wondered if they had fallen out.
They did not look a bit like a bride and
bridegroom off their wedding tour.

The next day Sir Arthur spent with
Messrs. Shane and Ucross at their office in
Garcin, and the following morning started
with Mr. Ucross for London. Wife and
mother saw him off, and afterwards, at the

latter's suggestion, they drove to what had
been the Castle Hill, to see the scene of
the landslip. What a change! Instead of
emerald turf, crowned with great trees, and
sloping down to the river, there stood a
perpendicular cliff of red gravel, and at its
foot a mass of ruin. Great oaks with their
roots in the air, and their branches buried,
dotted in here and there. In some places
the turf had slipped down with the soil
below it, and was still growing; in others
not a vestige of green appeared. The
choked-up river had now formed a lake
three hundred feet wide, its edges garnished
with rotting hedges. Here and there stood
a melancholy tree, bearing abnormal fruit,
stuck amongst its branches, and splitting
the current, which escaped by a cascade

over the *débris* of the Hill. Several small
streams which ran from the base of the
cliff told the reason of its fall. For years,
centuries perhaps, these silent sappers working in the gravel had been slowly, but
surely, undermining the hill, till at last it
cracked open and fell.

The two ladies got out of their carriage,
and one of them moved about on the heaps
of ruin, carefully examining as she went.

"I know what you are looking for, May,"
said (Gertrude) Lady Bellmonte, "but you
won't find it. It's buried."

"There were two," said May, looking up.

"Oh, that other thing does not count.
The real ones are buried, thank God !"

"So you believed in the legend after
all ?"

"I knew that it was a thing which made people uncomfortable. I was foolish enough to let it keep me in an agony of fear till I got your telegram, and yet I did not believe in it. I say, Thank God! because there is an end of the thing, true or false."

"Can you show me where poor Cowper was killed?" May asked.

"No; the place is under water now. It was down yonder near the ash-tree. I am afraid Arthur is right about that woman, his wife. She has gone off with some very valuable old lace I gave her to be mended, and I do not know where to write for it. I think I will drive round by her cottage on our way home, if you don't mind, and see if any of the neighbours have heard from her."

May did not mind. They drove round,

and, to their surprise, saw the cottage open, and Mrs. Cowper, dressed in the deepest weeds, sitting by the fire just as usual—sewing away upon that very lace.

"Why, Mrs. Cowper! I am surprised," began the elder lady. "Where have you been ?"

"To London," she answered, drily, "for advice."

"Ah, I see—about the child. How is he now ?"

"Much better, Lady Bellmonte. My son is much better than he has ever been. I have had excellent advice for him, and he will be better yet," said Gipsy Cowper's widow, calmly.

"I am glad to hear so good an account of him. I was a little hurt, Mrs. Cowper,

that you went away without letting me
know."

"Was your ladyship afraid about your
lace?"

"Well, I must say I did not like your
taking it away. It is very valuable—an
heir-loom of the Bellmontes—and really
belongs to you, my love," she explained,
turning to her daughter-in-law, "but I am
responsible for it."

"An heirloom of the Bellmontes!" Mrs.
Cowper repeated, passing her hand under
the beautiful old cobwebry, and holding it up to the light; "and therefore, it
really belongs to my niece, Sir Arthur's
wife."

"He was christened in part of it," his
mother continued, with a meaning smile,

" and perhaps that part need not be unmade.
Who knows what may happen ? "

" Who indeed ! " re-echoed Mrs. Cowper.
" Your ladyship may rest assured that this
Bellmonte heirloom will be quite safe with
me. I shall not go away again."

" When will you send it home ? "

" I will *bring* it home very soon," said
Mrs. Cowper.

" Well, that was lucky ! " observed the
elder Lady Bellmonte, as they resumed their
drive. " I am sorry I suspected her, and
especially that I mentioned my suspicions to
you. I really forgot that she was your aunt.
Do you think she was hurt ? "

" No ; but she was horrid," May replied.

"Well, I thought her as quiet and respectful as ever."

"In words, yes; but there was a bitterness—almost a threatening—in her tone and manner, which made me feel quite cold." May shivered.

"Nonsense, child!—threatening! Why, if it had not been for the work and recommendations I gave her, she would have starved when her husband was in jail, and now that the poor man is dead, she is even worse off. I thought her manner very nice and respectful. You must really think for yourself, dear, and not imbibe Arthur's prejudices. Don't you remember that she said she would *bring* the lace herself, when I asked her when she would send it?"

"Mamma dear, I cannot tell you how I

mistrust and dislike that woman, although she *is* my aunt."

"And yet you used to be kind to her."

"Yes, for Sib's sake; but that was before —before she said some things that—that I've been thinking about. Oh! I do so wish she had never come back."

"Then you'd have lost your lace," said the Dowager, smiling.

"I'd give all the lace in the world if—"

But here the carriage drew up at the Hall porch, and May made a rush for the post-bag, which had come in during their absence.

Sir Arthur returned on the following Saturday night, after an absence of four days, and both wife and mother were shocked by the change in his appearance.

"Oh! are you ill?" burst from both at once.

"No, darling—no, mother," he said; "not ill, but very tired and fagged. I've had a great deal of work and worry. I shall be better when I've had a bath; but don't wait dinner. Send me up something to May's room."

He drank three or four glasses of wine, one after the other, and sent the "something," tempting as it was, away almost untasted. Nor had the bath refreshed him up as he promised. He looked ten years older than when he left. There were lines of care on his handsome face, which completely changed its expression. If his hair had been cut short he would have borne a curious likeness to Gipsy Cowper, as he appeared that day when he snapped up young Dawkins.

May found him stretched on a lounge in front of the fire, and seated herself on a stool at his feet, just the reverse of the position in which we have seen them—a picture of health, and love, and hope—on the banks of the Minsterton river in the bright July sunshine. But it was black night now.

" Arthur dear," she said, " you have had bad news; share it with me. It is my right. You shall not suffer alone. Tell me what has happened ! I am brave enough to bear anything—with you."

" You will be brave indeed, my darling, if you can bear what—what every one will know on Monday," he groaned.

" I am your true wife, Arthur. I did not

suppose when we married that our life would be one long honeymoon. No matter what has happened, you are my dear, good, noble husband; nothing can change our love."

"God bless you for that!" he cried. "Well, my poor pet, the most extraordinary thing has happened."

She nestled closer to him, threw her arms round his knees, and hid her face in them.

"A claimant," he continued, "has appeared for the Bellmonte estates—all of them—everything that I thought mine. Do you follow me?"

The golden head nodded twice.

"If his case be true, neither I nor my father had any right to be here. Just think what that means. Suppose my father had

no right to make the provision he did for my
mother ?   Suppose that I had no right to
anything ?   We should be beggars.   At this
moment, my mother would not possess a
penny. I should be ruined. You cannot
realize it, May ; you are not listening."

Her arms closed tighter, and the nestling
head bent again.

"We should be expelled from our dear
old home; we should be cast adrift on the
world as impostors who had fattened for
years on what was not their own. Why
the very clothes we wear are—would not be
our own !   What would become of us ?
What could I do without a profession, or a
trade, or perhaps a friend in my adversity ?"

His hand fell instinctively on her bright
curls, and manly tears dimmed their gold.

"All this would be so if that claim is true—and, and—oh my wife! my darling! I fear it is true. May, you *cannot* be listen-ing (reproachfully). Do you hear me SAY that I fear it is true?"

For the first time the hidden face was turned up to his.

"I know it is," she said softly.

"You—know—it—is!" he cried, starting back as far as her arms would let him.

"Yes, dear Arthur, I knew it months before our marriage."

"Then in heaven's name! why did you marry me?"

"*Because I loved you!*" broke from the tender, trembling lips.

Because I loved you! shone from the eager, honest eyes.

Because I loved you! beamed from every line in the dear, true face.

"Why, oh why did you not trust me?" he cried.

"I was afraid. I thought that what men call honour would have made you give me up because you would be poor; and then I should not have been yours to help you when the trouble came. Don't say beggars, dear; we have more left to live on than the Prices, and see how happy they are."

"It was for fear of this, then, that you have been saving your money?" he asked suddenly.

"Yes, Arthur."

"And I called her mean!" he muttered through his clenched teeth, throwing up his arms, as though to invoke a punishment for his crime.

"Dear Arthur, I did it for the best."

"The best!—you have done everything for the best. I see it all now. For this you get me to travel without servants, and rough it; for this you have been showing me in every way how to be content and happy in small means; for this you refused a settlement out of the estate, and secured the little patrimony I had independent of it, against the evil day when the crash might come. What a clear head!—what a loving heart! Now God be praised for this," he said solemnly; "it takes out half the sting —you noble wife!—you true, true woman!"

"No!" she cried, starting from the arms which longed to enfold her; "don't touch

me—don't look at me. I am *not* noble; I
am *not* true. Arthur, when first we met at
Minsterton I deliberately laid a snare to
catch you, for your rank, for your money.
I did not love you—oh, the shame, the
shame of it! I kissed you as I used to kiss
my doll when I was a child. I smiled in
your face, and lied. My uncle knew all
about us, and helped me. We had a plan
to inveigle you into a secret marriage, and
then shame your father into pardoning you.
I made it up—not he; he was not bad
enough for that. No, listen; but you must
not blame Sib. She thought, as you did,
that our meetings were kept from uncle.
She never knew—she does not now know—
his share in it. He put me up to writing
to you so that you should be betrayed into

III.   44

a promise upon which we could sue you at law if you did not keep your word. *You* not keep your word! Oh, Arthur! there is not a woman in all this world more basely cunning, more coldly, sordidly false than I was. I encouraged that creature, Duff. For weeks I wavered between you, caring not one straw for either; but deliberating which would give me the richer spoil. Fancy what I must have been when I hesitated between you and—Duff! My uncle favoured him, as I told you. That was true; and one day, sure of his conquest, he kissed me. I lied when I told you I had escaped the touch of his hot, hateful lips. He *did* kiss me; and from that instant I began to love you, my own, my king!—and every throb of my heart for you was a lash,

and every caress you gave me was a reproach; and the more dear you became to
me the more I hated my wicked, wicked
self. I would have confessed all before we
married; but I loved you so, and I could
not bear it—I loved you so. I thought
that when I was your wife, and had proved
to you how changed I was, I could show
you my old, bad self, and we would bury
it; but oh! the wearing, gnawing fear that
you would find her without my aid; that
some one—uncle, Mr. Duff—would betray
me, and you would never believe I married
you for yourself, my darling! At last I
discovered this secret; and, Arthur, I almost
rejoiced over it; for I knew then I could
prove I was true at last. Arthur, husband!
tell me you believe that I was true at last!"

"I know not what to believe now," he replied bitterly. "Ten minutes ago you might have told me anything, and I would have believed it. How am I to know now that you really were in possession of this secret. This may be some other plot; some scheme to rid yourself of a broken man. Do you want me to say something in sudden anger that will give you an excuse for demanding a separation now I am ruined? Bah! it is too flimsy. How could you know what was unknown to every one save that loyal, always true, always faithful heart, whose last thought was for my good? Ah, generous and happy!—if we could only have changed places! If the evil of our race had fallen upon me instead of you that day, it would have been a lighter blow than this."

May arose from where she knelt, sobbing as though her heart would burst, unlocked her desk, and placed the paper she had found in the great library in her husband's hand.

CHAPTER IV.

RE BELLMONTE.

NORMAN DRUMMOND did not return to his chambers that evening when he left his wife with that carelessly-uttered, "I suppose so," ringing in her brain. It was true that he had an important case to get up, but he knew his mind was not his own to think with, just now. It would run on the cowardly work he had begun. It would go back to the woman he had wronged, and wonder how the misery he had left "to soak" was affecting her. He felt very

much as might a poisoner who had left some
deadly drug to be taken by his victim; but
did not know the moment when it would
begin its work—or end it;—who had fled
from the sight of the death he had dealt,
and yet longed to have the horrid assurance
before his eyes. This man had killed a
woman's peace of mind, and was haunted
by its dying agonies. He must do something to distract his thoughts, and what
should that be? Go to a theatre? He
tried it, and stumbled upon a play in which
something very like his own case formed the
plot. It angered him to notice that all the
sympathies of the audience were with the
deceived woman. He thought that people—
utter strangers—looked at him as though
they would say, " There! that's what ought

to happen to men like *you!*" and he left the place in disgust. Then he remembered it was Mr. Angus Duff's reception - night. There would be company of the sort he required, and other things to drown thought, in that gentleman's splendid rooms; so thither he hastened.

Mr. Duff had taken May's jilting very much to heart, and he, too, had sought to drown his troubles in excitement. He found consolation—or what he took for it—where many another man who has failed with a pure woman, seeks it; and the supply was equal to the demand. Every Thursday, from ten o'clock till any hour next morning, he kept open house to agreeable persons of both sexes, and made it all right with the police, if not with his neighbours. There was a little whist, a little loo (unlimited), and a good deal of champagne. Drummond had only assisted once before at these meetings, and then had left early, not at all pleased with his company or the means provided for his entertainment. And he left unrequited. " A stuck-up cad," said the men. One of the ladies remarked that he must be a Moody and Sankey, and as that was enough to raise a roar of laughter, you may judge for yourself what sort of wit prevailed.

To-night, therefore, he entered rather under a cloud. He soon dispelled it. He drank freely, he played deeply, he laughed loudly. The same lady who had branded him with Methodism, pronounced him "quite too much of a dear." When he let himself into his gloomy chambers as the clocks were striking three, he was desperate with drink and excitement. He sat down to his desk, and in an unsteady hand wrote this letter, to be posted when decent folks should be about:

" Dear Sib,

" We made a mistake about McBhale's house. It is on the English side of the road. This need make no difference, if you will only take a reasonable view of things, and let them stay as they are.

" Your's,

" Norman."

He folded, directed, and stamped it; and placed it in the box marked " For the post " in the clerk's room, so that it should be sent off the first thing after the arrival of that functionary. Then he flattered himself that he had got the whole thing off his mind. There would be some tears he need not see, and some reproaches he would not have to hear. They would probably not meet again. She would write to him, of course, and he almost winced at the thought of what might be placed on paper for him. And there it would end. The idea that she would be content to let things stay as they were, and live as his mistress, never crossed his mind. He knew her too well to think that. He cared for her too little now to hope it. What a fool he had been! He laughed at the old dream-begotten phantasy which had connected her with Garcin Hall, and all its grandeur. If his plot against Arthur Bellmonte had succeeded; if Sir Alexander had made him his heir; why then he might have afforded to marry a splendidly-handsome wife, just as he could have afforded to have splendidly-handsome hunters, and pictures, and what not. All that had vanished. What he wanted now was freedom; to be quit of the millstone which a moment of passion had fastened round his neck; to live for himself, and rise with the tide which was floating him on to Fortune.

He awoke late, with a head by no means in condition to tackle that important case. Luckily he had nothing in court that day, and could give it his whole attention. As he entered his working-room, he saw his clerk in the act of placing some new papers on the table.

" From Boyle and Clerk, sir," said the

man, "delivered this morning. Mr. Clerk's compliments, and the matter is pressing. Would like to have your opinion as soon as possible." His master glanced at the brief. It was endorsed " *Re Bellmonte* case for the opinion of Mr. Drummond. Twenty guineas. *Very pressing.*"

For a moment his heart smote him. Boyle and Clerk were Sir Arthur's private attorneys, and he owed their briefs entirely to his recommendation. If he knew what the post was carrying to Chelsea? Well, business is business. He untied the tape and began to read this pressing matter.

Ten minutes had scarcely past when he sounded his bell for the clerk.

" Have you posted that letter I put in the box last night."

" Yes, sir."

" When ? "

" Two hours ago."

" Run to the office and get it back ; I've made a mistake. I've used the wrong envelope. Don't stand gaping there, man ! run ! "

" But it is contrary to the regulations."

" The regulations be d—; get it. Spend twenty pounds, but get it," thundered Drummond.

It was not to be got for all the money in the Bank of England. It had gone on its way the honest course of the post, and the Queen herself could not intercept it.

Drummond seized his hat and dashed off into Fleet Street. "Cheyne Walk, Chelsea ! " he shouted to the driver of the first hansom he saw. "Take that," tossing a sovereign, " and drive like mad."

" Where's your mistress ?" he asked, when his door was opened to him.

" Oh, if you please, sir, she's not at home," said the servant, who appeared to be in a flutter of fright.

" Has the post come in ?"

" Yes, sir.

" Give me the letters."

" Oh, if you please, sir, there ain't none."

" Are you sure ?"

" Yes, sir — leastwise there ain't none *now*. Mr. Tyrell come and fetched them away."

" How dared you give him your mistress's letters ?"

"If you please, sir, she told me to when she went away last night."

Drummond staggered into the hall and threw himself upon a seat.

"Went away last night!" he gasped, wiping the cold perspiration from his brows.

"Yes, sir, she were very ill soon after you left. And then she went out and came back, and went out again with nothing but her travelling-bag, and then she said, 'Anne,' she said, 'I expect a letter from Lady Bell-monte to-morrow. If Mr. Tyrell calls, give it to him, and any other,' and that's all I know. If you was to bring me a stack of Bibles, I'd swear to it."

Another Hansom and another big fare to the office of the *Orny And,* where he found Tom Tyrell.

"They tell me at the house that you called this morning for my wife's letters," he said in his old superior style. "I wrote to her last night, not thinking she would start so soon. It is of no importance now; please give it me."

Tom Tyrell turned on him his foxiest look.

"So you said you wrote a letter to your wife, did you?" laying an emphasis on the *wife*.

"I did, and I want it."

"You'll *have* to want it."

"No nonsense, Mr. Tyrell. I don't know why you should have been called upon to interfere between us, but this I am sure of —I am entitled to any letter addressed to my wife, and this being one written to her by

III. 45

myself, no one can pretend to keep it from me."

"That you can settle between yourselves, when you've settled something else," said Tom Tyrell in his grimmest tone.

"I never was much in love with Sib Cowper, but I'm damned if I don't stand up for her against such a scoundrel as you are."

"Take care."

"Oh, I'm not afraid. She came to me last night as her only friend. She must have been hard pressed when she came to me, and she told me what she feared. I couldn't answer her question. I am not so well up in geography as that, and so she's gone to find out the truth for herself.'

"Gone to Scotland?" Drummond exclaimed.

"I hope she hasn't," Tom replied. "I hope it will turn out that the place is in England, and so that she can get rid of you. She's a d— fine woman, is Sib, and deserves a better life than you could give her."

"She is labouring under a most absurd delusion, Mr. Tyrell; some careless expression of mine, for which I am very sorry, has led her to think I doubt the validity of our marriage. There is no doubt about it."

"Did you tell her so in that letter?"

"I—I did; but I must be more explicit now. Give it to me, and I will write another here, in your presence if you like, telling her she perfectly misunderstood me.

Nay; I'll go after her and tell her so, and give her the letter myself."

"That seems fair enough," said Tom, apparently mollified, but the fox was dodging all around the corners of his mouth as he spoke. "Still, to make all sure, I'll open that letter and mark it so as to be certain that the one you wrote last night is the one she'll get to-morrow."

"I allow no one to open my letters to my wife, Mr. Tyrell," said Drummond in his lofty tone.

"And I allow no one to touch my niece's correspondence," he replied with a grin. "I know you fine gentlemen; you don't ride the high horse over me. You've played fast and loose with that poor girl, and now for some reason or other—I don't know what,

but I *will* know—you want to play loose
and fast. I tell you that Sib Cowper, or
Sib Drummond, whatever she may be, has
gone off to see for herself if that place where
you pretended to marry her, Scotch fashion,
is in Scotland or no. What do you want
with any letter you wrote last night? What
do you gain by stopping here and jawing
about it? Why don't you start after
her at once, if you can face her and explain matters, and leave the letter here to
prove you've had no after-thought about
it?"

"Because I will not be dictated to."

"All right. Go your own way, and I'll
take mine."

"Will you show me that letter?"

"For you to snatch it? No; you're a

younger and a stronger man than I am, but I am no fool."

" Then I must see what the law will do."

" The law ! Do you want to wash your dirty linen in a Police Court ? "

" There is no dirty linen, as you call it. I should not at all object, if you force me to do it, to claim my wife's property from a stranger, as you are, anywhere."

" And so acknowledge the legality of your marriage ? "

" Most assuredly."

" Now I *know* there's something up," said Tom Tyrell. " Out with it, man. Tell the whole truth, and perhaps I'll help you."

He could not tell the truth. It was too bad, too despicable. He slunk out of the room, muttering something about his attorney, and left Tom Tyrell master of the situation—and the letter.

"They are a pair," he growled when left to himself. "A pair of high-falooting wind-bags; but I've been hard on Sib. To think of her coming to me! I never could like that fellow with his grand airs, and his curly smile. She has a woman's instincts about him, and I've a man's. But why the devil does he tell her last night he *supposes* they are married, and to-day talks big to me about her being his wife?"

Mr. Drummond did not go to any attorney. He knew better. He returned to his chambers and finished the perusal of Messrs. Boyle and Clerk's pressing brief. It told him that the widow of the late Sir George Bellmonte, *alias* George Cowper, as

the next friend of his only son, had laid
claim to the Bellmonte estates; it placed
before him a copy of the paper which May
had found, and it requested his opinion
whether Sir Arthur had a leg to stand
upon.   It did not use those words, but
that was the pith of it.   So here he was
with nothing but the life of a puny, crippled,
epileptic child between him and Garcin
Hall, with all its glories, as the husband of
its presumptive heiress—Sibyl !   Sir George
Bellmonte's (*alias* Cowper's) only daughter !

And he had told her he " supposed " they
were man and wife, and had written—what?
His head was in a muddle when he wrote.
It was more confused when he tried to
remember what he had written.   All he
knew for certain, was, that he had told her

McPhale's house was on the wrong, *i. e.* the English, side of the road. But for that cursed letter the dreams he had dreamed might come true. What had he told her? That his father did not recognize civil marriage—well, did that alter the law? That a second ceremony might give rise to ugly surmises—was that not so? That he "supposed" the scene of their union was in a country where it was valid—of course he *supposed* it was, or he would not have done what he did. Everything would be smoothed down and explained away, and made right; he would marry her a dozen times if she liked; all could be made right except that cursed letter which Tom Tyrell the blackguard!—(he liked to think him a blackguard; it was a sort of

hedge against his own miscoloured fleece)—
held, and no cajoling or blustering could
get it out of his clutches. As he pondered,
it suddenly struck him that bullying and
cajoling are not the only means to be
employed in the premises, or the most likely
ones to succeed. So about four o'clock he
again sought Tom Tyrell, and after some
difficulty in the outer office was admitted.

" Well," said Tom, looking up from his
writing, " what now ? "

" This," replied Drummond. " I'll give
you two hundred pounds for that letter."

" What ! " shouted Tom, starting up.

" Two hundred pounds, half down in
bank-notes, and the rest in a cheque payable
this day month."

" Don't play the fool."

"I'm serious. See, here is the first hundred in bank notes," and he produced five crisp new bills of twenty pounds each.

"I suppose I'm going to make an ass of myself," growled Tyrell, "as I always do when there's a woman about. I want some money badly just now, and that ungrateful stuck-up May won't help me; but I must be honest with Sib."

"Two hundred pounds," Drummond repeated, "for you, and no harm to anybody."

"Say that again. No harm to Sib?"

"On the contrary—in the long run."

Tom unlocked a drawer, and took out two letters, both addressed to Mrs. Drummond at Chelsea, and both re-directed to "*The Hall, Garcin, Hopshire,*" in his own not particularly-clear handwriting. "Got a telegram just before you came in," he explained. She's going to her precious May. One of these is from her (turning the letters over and over); do you know which is which?"

"That is mine—the thin one," Drummond replied quickly, and stretched out his hand.

"Stop a bit. Let's see the postmarks. *Fleet Street*, and this *Garcin*. All right. Now, why don't you want Sib to get this?"

"Because I wish to avoid a fuss—there!"

"And it's worth two hundred pounds! Lord! you're right though. Give a woman a grievance and she'll slice it as thin, and make it go as far, as a luncheon-bar. Hem, you're right! You shall have it, but, look ye here, you're not going to get me into a fuss to save yourself from one? Suppose

I pop this letter into the fire just as it is ? "

" I'd rather you would give it to me."

" Yes, and have Sib's tongue let loose on me for the rest of my natural life. Perhaps you know how d— cutting she can be. Besides, I promised her to keep her letters from you. Is there money in it or anything you want to keep ? "

" No ; nothing."

" Then I can say you came here and said she was making a mistake, and were going to tell her so, and therefore I just pitched it into the fire, thinking it was no good—will that do ? "

" Well, perhaps it will."

" No perhapses. Will it earn that two hundred ? "

"Yes."

"Honour?"

"I have said so, Mr. Tyrell. My word is enough; but there are the notes as you are so sus— particular."

"Good. So *there*, and *there*, and *there*."

With the first "there," Tyrell tore the letter in two; with the second he put the pieces together and tore it into four; and with the third he dropped them into the fire. It shot up, and turned the paper into flame; into black, gold-spangled clouds; into fine gray ashes; into the red glow which lined its caverns into which it mingled, and was lost as though it had never been. Norman Drummond gave a sigh of relief as the cleansing fire did its work.

So did Tom Tyrell when the notes were safe in his pocket.

CHAPTER V.

RUIN.

WE left May Bellmontc in the act of handing her husband the paper which was to prove her pre-knowledge of the claim which might turn him out of doors.

We left him so crushed by the revelations which she had previously made that he had not sense to sift the wheat from the chaff, and to see the truth reflected in the very falsehoods she confessed. His doubts stung down her sobs, and quenched her tears. She stood erect by his side now, the more composed of the two. He had sunk moodily into a seat, buried his face in his hands, and pushed the paper from him. It was plainly written, in a large free hand, and the ink had not much faded.

"I do not want to read anything, now," he said; "I don't think I *could*, if I tried. Things jump about so before my eyes."

"You must read it, Arthur. It is bad enough for me to have to confess my wickedness towards you, but not to be believed when I—Arthur! for God's sake look up; rouse yourself. You say that no one could have known this secret beside George Cowper. Do you understand what that implies? Don't you see that you are accusing me of rank idiotcy? Why should I pretend to have known before our wedding that you might be dispossessed of all you had? What good would that do me, if I were the woman you suppose? If, after all, I sold myself for a title, or wealth, shouldn't I grieve for them now that they are all but lost? Shouldn't I reproach you with imposture, say that *you* must have known it all along, that *you* had deceived me. Why, Arty! how can you be so stupid? If you cannot read this let me read it for you. It is a letter written by your Uncle George to your father."

"Ah!" he said, clenching his teeth, "I should like to know what my Uncle George had to say to my father. Read it to me; my head swims."

Here is the letter:

III. 46

Garcin, May 19th.

" MY DEAR BROTHER,

"I CAME here on business last Tuesday for a day, as I hoped, but am detained by one of my nervous attacks. The doctors call them so, but they feel to me unpleasantly like incipient paralysis. This is all the worse, because I have something on my conscience which the approach of death requires me to remove. That boy that you have seen at my London house, called George Cowper, is my legitimate son. I married his mother in Teddington Church, and he was born in a cottage I had there by the river. You can verify this at your leisure. You will find my signature on the registers. The boy is a scamp; perhaps that is partly my fault. My reason for not acknowledging him was that I thought I might marry again, and because his mother gave me no reason to be proud of him. She ran away from him and me, and went to the bad. In a will, which I mean to revoke, I gave him five thousand pounds, and left the estates to go to you. I feel that I could not die easy without doing more than that. He must have his rights, and I will not be unjust to you who have considered yourself my heir. I have sent for Ucross, and he will be here to-morrow to draw me a new will. I shall give the lands to George, and create a rent charge on them of two thousand five hundred pounds a-year, for you and your boy after you. You are a just man, Alex., so put yourself in my place, and do not judge me harshly.

"I shall keep this letter open till the will is signed."

"That is all, Arthur," said May, returning him the paper. "I suppose he did not live to finish it."

"How came it into your possession?"

"I found it the day I was taken ill, before you came. I was searching in the library for a book which Mr. Moule wanted, and I knocked down some big volumes, out of one of which it fell. Perhaps I ought not to have read it, but how was I to know what it contained? I began to see what ought to be done with it, and the mischief was done before I knew there was any. Then I fainted, and lay there I don't know how long in the cold."

"Poor childie!" he said, laying his hand on her head. The touch thrilled her.

"Oh!" she burst forth joyfully, "you do believe me now?"

"You must give me time," he said. "I'm not quick and clever like some fellows; I can't take it all in just now. It seems as though great happiness, or great misery, had fallen on me; and I don't know clearly which it is. Found it the day she was taken ill, before I came!" he repeated to himself— then turning to her he demanded, "How did you know it was in my Uncle George's hand-writing?"

"I guessed that."

"You were right," he observed, taking up the letter and examining it. "He did not live to give instructions for that will he

speaks of.   He was found in the library
struck with paralysis one night, and he died
the next day."

"Can you account for the letter getting
into that book ? "

"I suppose he put it there himself.   It
does not matter.   And you knew this when
you married me ! "

"I did, and when Uncle Tyrell wrote
that a man had been killed by the land-slip
I knew who it was."

"I think I see what you mean.   You
believe in the legend of the Sinking Stones ? "

"Arty dear, how can one disbelieve it
now ?   The non-sinking at your father's
death is accounted for, and when the real
head of the house came to a sudden end
they had a sudden fall."

"Say rather that their sudden fall caused his sudden death. It's a coincidence—nothing more. Now for another question. —You had that paper safe; how could you tell that any one else possessed a clue to the secret?"

"From something which my Aunt, Mrs. Cowper, told me. I thought nothing of it at the time, but it formed afterwards. She told me that once or twice when her husband came home tipsy he pretended he had only to say the word to be a gentleman."

"He *was* a gentleman at heart," said Arthur. "He knew his rights and would not claim them. Mr. Moule has told me all about it. If he had lived another hour he would have destroyed the packet con-

taining the proofs of his birth, and that
vixen wife of his would never have gained
the right clue.   But he died, and it was only
his dead body that gave up the secret.   I
have been to my lawyers in London, and
we have examined the registers at Teddington.   These left very little hope, and what
there was is quenched by Sir George's letter.
I cannot resist."

"I know now," May mused, "what Aunt
Milly meant when she said she would bring
the lace home herself, very soon."

On the following Monday the tenants on
the Bellmonte and Garcin estates received
notice not to pay their rents to any one but
the guardian of Sir George Bellmonte, or
her duly-appointed agent ; and the signature
was "Amelia, Lady Bellmonte."   The news

spread like wild-fire, and it was curious to observe how many people knew it all along. Gipsy Cowper had committed—some said a perjury, others a murder—and old Sir Alexander knew all about it, and had him in his power. That was the reason why the one was excluded from the succession and the other allowed to inherit title and estate. Young Sir Arthur inherited the secret, so he also could keep the rightful heir from his own. This was why the latter got Wrenshaw's farm, and was forgiven, and excused, and defended for his numerous rascalities. Why, it stood to reason ! I notice that many things which will not stand on their own bottoms are made to stand to reason. At last—so these wiseacres had it—he had got reckless and determined to assert his rights;

made poor Mr. Moule give him up the packet—don't you see ?—which contained the proofs, and the very next morning he would have broken his oath, and put the law in force against his benefactor's son. But the hand of Providence was raised and smote him.

There was a good deal of talk about the hand of Providence, as though it were the hand of some clock which the speaker regulated by his own watch, and wound up every Sunday. The legend of the Sinking Stones got about again, and gave rise to much animated discussion. Some took Arthur Bellmonte's view, that it was the fall of the hill (including the stones upon its crest) that caused Cowper's death, and not Cowper's impending death which caused the fall of the hill. Had a common process of nature been working, for centuries perhaps, for the express purpose of undermining Castle Hill, so that it would crack open on the very day Cowper regained his papers? Why, it was absurd! On the other side, those many strange cases of fulfilment were triumphantly quoted. And here was another! Nothing short of a cataclysm, such as actually took place, could have caused the stones to sink, supported as they were by the solid foundations of the old Norman Tower. There was nothing to show that the undermining had been going on for centuries—and if it had, why, so also had the curse! On the contrary, the deceased man, who knew the river better than any one else in the whole county, had observed,

whilst fishing shortly before the slip, that
the current through Poynder's hole had
changed its course. It used to run under
the bank towards the hill—it then ran out
from both. His time had come to die, and
the stones had to sink. Did they fall on
him? No! They lie buried two hundred
yards from the spot where he was thrown
down.

So there were the *post hocs*, and the
propter hocs, and the latter were split
amongst themselves into two factions,
the *Finalities* and the *Anti-Finalities;* the
former contended that the curse had
come to an end because there were no
more stones to sink; the latter held that
it could not end as long as there were
Bellmontes alive—that the race and its old

stronghold would disappear together, and
these, with Mr. Moule at their head, pointed
with triumph to what Sir Alexander had
called the "doubtful stone," which remained
intact on the verge of the chasm which the
slip had caused. Mr. Moule wrote a learned
lecture on that stone, and disposed of all
his former patron's doubts repecting it. It
was part of a gargoyle, was of earlier
workmanship than anything about the
Abbey, and was undoubtedly—so he concluded—a portion of the tower. Upon one
thing, and one thing only, did all agree,
and that was that Sir George Bellmonte,
alias Cowper, was dead, and nothing could
defeat the claim of his son.

Nothing could. Arthur took counsel's
opinion, as a matter of form, but the proofs

contained in the packet which had so nearly gone to the bottom of Poynder's hole, corroborated by Sir George's unfinished letter, were irresistible. Counsel—that is to say, Mr. Drummond—suggested a compromise, and Messrs. Boyle and Clerk, assisted by Shane and Ucross, did their best to force one on.

"Of course we shall fight you," they told the other side; "and as we are in possession, and have all the sinews of war, the fight will be a hard and a long one."

The reply came from Amelia Lady Bellmonte herself. "If," she wrote, "Mr. Arthur Bellmonte thinks it consistent with the character of a gentleman to resist the rights of an orphan with that orphan's own money, he can do so. As my son's guardian I cannot, and as his mother I will not, renounce an acre or a shilling."

This stung Arthur to the quick. The idea of depending upon position and wealth to defeat a poor adversary was bad enough; but to *keep* him poor, and use the weapons which ought to be his own, against him, was simply unbearable to his upright mind. Are you angry with him for not taking his wife to his heart, and blotting out her former untruthfulness with happy tears shed over her latter loyalty? It was better for them both that he took time to think it over—that he was hard to convince at first —for when forgiveness did come, it was full and complete.

He had no difficulty in satisfying her that a contest was not only useless, but dishonourable. The trouble was with his mother. She—poor lady!—was very hard to convince. It was not justice — it could not be law. The creature (meaning the once irreproachable Mrs. Cowper) must be out of her mind. If Arthur had one spark of love left for his wretched mother he would resist. She would resist to the very last, and he had no right to sacrifice her interests by yielding. With much difficulty it was explained to her that she had no interests. Her dead husband's will was a piece of paper—no more. He had nothing of his own to leave her. It was by right all George Cowper's, and all that had been George Cowper's was now his heir's, exactly as though he had himself claimed it on Sir George's death. It was hard upon her—

very hard. A woman grows to a place she loves, faster and deeper than we men do. She throws out a thousand tender roots that we know nothing of. She has not, as a rule, those fine instincts of justice which sometimes rob calamity of its sting. It strikes her with its full, bitter force. Eleven happy years had she lived at Garcin Hall as its mistress. There had she seen her handsome boy expand, body and mind, into manhood. There she had closed his father's eyes, and borne the blank, bitter loneliness of widowhood. There she had welcomed the bride of her only son, and looked forward to renew her life with another generation on her knee.

And she would have to leave it! Leave the grand old rooms she loved; the quaint

I II. 47

relics of bygone ages she so prized and
cared for; the old pictures that had smiled
on her all those years; the trees and flowers
she had planted with her own hands; the
poor to whom she had been a mother and a
friend! She must leave them all!—title—
position—wealth—for no fault that she had
committed. It was very—very hard.

But it was right, and it was inevitable.
I want this distinctly understood. There
are no forged papers, no substituted children, and only one doubtful marriage in all
this story. The poor little cripple we know
of was veritably Sir George Bellmonte of
Garcin, and likely to remain so for many
years. The advice he got in London was
chiefly legal, but he had other assistance;
and his mother was correct, both ways,

when she said he was better than he ever
had been, and would be better yet.

In the midst of all this sorrow came a
new distress. Sib arrived, weary with her
long journey, wretched with the horrid truths
it had taught her, looking the ghost of her
former self, and seeking shelter of those who
had no home, and comfort from the comfort-
less! She had discovered that McPhale's
house was indeed on the wrong side of the
boundary ; that she was not a wife, and that
the man she had loved with all the strength
and purity of her heart, was weary of her.
That was the hardest blow of all.

Of course she knew nothing of the pend-
ing eviction of the Bellmontes. She rushed
to May with the instinct of love ; no reproach on her lips, no idea of holding her to

any shade of responsibility for her part in
the miserable farce she had advocated—in
her mind. Only because she loved her; and
when she found that she had brought fresh
sorrow, she was eager to fly again—anywhere. But this neither Arthur nor his
wife would hear of. It was a great blow
to May, who alternated between self-con-
demnation and self-defence. If she had
only been half as careful about her geography
as she had been about her law! But as is
so often the case, having got one thing
exact, she made all the others fit to suit it.
She asked Scotchmen and Scotchwomen if
they were in Scotland; and they had
answered, according to their lights, that
they were. What could she have done
more? Surely they knew best, as they

lived on the spot. She had to learn that
those who live " on the spot " are usually
the worst possible authorities about it,
especially when their prejudices are in-
volved. If she had gone a mile further
north and had asked an Englishman, " Is
this England ? " he would have told her,
" Yes, to be sure ; " and if she had gone a
mile further south and asked a Scot, " Is
this Scotland ? " he would have answered
there was " na doot aboot it." Anywhere
in the proximity of towns, or in land having
a value which brought it within the clutch
of the law for taxation, the line is drawn
clearly enough ; but out there on a blank
waste of marsh and heather, too poor for even
a grouse, with any self-respect, to live on—
who knew, and who cared to learn, where it

ran? Certainly not Mr. McPhale, who being canny in his generation, played off Scotch tax-collectors against their English brethren, and was on the other side for whichever came " wi' his papers and things speering aboot his dues."

May's vexation with herself did not make her spare Drummond. The proposition came from him; *he* ought to have made sure; he knew it—the cold-blooded wretch! " If I were a man," she said, with flashing eyes, " I'd kill him." For a good hater commend me to a tender-hearted woman: and it was well perhaps for Mr. Norman Drummond that his wife's warmest friend was of her own sex, and that he lived in days when ladies do not find champions to carry out their will in such matters. She was furious

with Arthur because, loyal to a man who, as
he thought, had been his friend, he suggested
that the culprit had not yet been heard, and
that there might be some mistake. "What
mistake could there be? Had he not neglected her, made her unhappy, gone abroad
and left her, concealed his marriage from
family and friends, and refused to make her
amends? And to think that after all it
was his own flesh and blood that he had
wronged! Sibyl was the daughter of Norman
Drummond's first cousin, since both he and
George Cowper were the children of Bellmontes—the one of the daughter Cecilia,
the other of her brother, the head of the
house, the late Sir George. Norman would
be thoroughly ashamed of himself, now
the truth about Sib's relationship to him-

self has come out." — Thus indignant
May.

Sib did her best to silence these discussions, unmindful that they really did the
disputants good.   There is no better pallia-
tive for your own troubles than the troubles
of others, when you can sympathise with
them.   In the broad glare of her dear Sib's
grief, May's own pain cast a softening
shadow.

CHAPTER VI.

SIR GEORGE AT HOME.

THE ground was lightly spread with snow, which glittered on the leaves of the evergreens, and outlined with a sharper touch the great bare limbs of the Garcin elms. The winter sun loomed red and low in a dull blue sky ; and there was that peculiar stillness in the air which comes with frost. You could hear the *drip! drip! drip!* of the melting icicles where the sunbeams fell through the trees, and a sound like sobbing went up from the earth as though the land were grieving.

A hack-carriage from the railway station
stood at the side-entrance of the Hall, and
soon it was entered by three weeping
women. Then a man came out hurriedly,
took his place by May's side, and they were
driven off.

"Four for London—no, thank you, Mr.
Badger—second-class," said Arthur, with a
a smile (but he has to set his teeth hard).
"We are poor people now."

About this time a chariot and pair dashed
up to the main entrance of the Hall. Two
new footmen hastened to open the door; a
new butler (*vice* Mr. Bins) was on the steps;
a new housekeeper a little way behind him;
and in her rear a row of new servants were
drawn up in double file. All this had been
arranged and rehearsed by the new butler,

and was very well done. Through this
phalanx — bowing right and left — passed
Amelia Lady Bellmonte, leading by the
hand a pale boy, slightly misshapen. Both
were clad in the deepest mourning, and one
was quivering with the deepest joy. Judged
by her manner, she might have been in the
position of a lady all her life. She swept
along, flung a few orders over her shoulder,
and made for what was the former Lady Bellmonte's boudoir. Here she hurriedly closed
the door, sunk down on her knees, clasped
the boy to her heart, and gasped, *At last!* "

This was her reward for her patient,
indomitable pursuit of one idea. When she
married George Cowper she had not the
least suspicion that he was even a relative
of the Bellmontes, or other than what he

appeared to be—a man of fashion, with unlimited resources, and friends in high posi-
tions. How he slid down from this estate
we know from his own lips. The subse-
quent drunken boasts that he could be a
gentleman if he chose, was only one of
many hints which his wife stored up in her
memory. When, on the day they parted,
he turned pale and trembled at her reminder
of what he had said on those occasions, she
knew that it was not mere drunken brag.
He had something to conceal ; he was eager
to know how much he had disclosed. Still
she knew not in what direction to look for
the clue, till one day she went to the Hall
with some work for Lady Bellmonte, and
found her in the library. There, by mere
chance, her eye fell on Sir George's portrait

—the portrait which May had asked, "Who have I seen so like you?" and the truth flashed into her mind. From that day she kept an incessant watch. She gained over Mr. Moule's housekeeper and the old woman who cooked for her husband. Jealousy was the excuse given, and in this cause her charming sex listened and spied with delightful activity—not so much for the satisfaction of confounding the man, as for the pleasure and triumph to be gained by exposing his hussy. He had no hussy; but there was a mysterious packet which he and Mr. Moule talked about, and which Mr. Moule did not want to keep. "It's money, I'll be bound," said the spy; "money as he's keeping you out of for spite." Her employer encouraged this idea, and bade her

keep a bright look-out for that packet.
With the connivance of the other detective,
Mrs. Cowper visited her husband's house
several times during his absence at the
dredging works, and had a good search.
He was a careless man, and might leave
things about; but she found nothing. On
the day of the land-slip, Mr. Moule's domestic
reported that he had gone out fishing, and
taken the packet with him. Now or never
was the time. She had no defined plan at
starting. She would hide herself in the
house, and take her chance. Thus was her
early presence on the scene of the catastrophe at Castle Hill accounted for. The
day after her husband's funeral she went to
London and verified the statements made in
the papers which she had found on his body.

Then she hunted up a lawyer who was willing to take up her case upon speculation, and a first-rate speculation it turned out. We know the rest. There stood the head of the house of Bellmonte—that pale, rickety boy, who could not be made to understand why he was here—and there was his mother on her knees, almost worshipping him! For him lived the one generous movement of her heart—he was afflicted, and his necessity for maternal love had planted that divine emotion in her breast. Through him all its long pent-up bitterness flowed free. Ah! what a weapon he had become for humbling those she hated.

It so happened that many of those persons were there assembled in Vehmgericht at Lady Louisa Dunbrogue's five o'clock tea, to discuss what society was to do about those other Bellmontes—(the new-comers were known as those *other* Bellmontes, with a curl of the lip over the "*other*"). How it would have delighted the other lady to have been present (invisible) and heard the president sum up.

"My dears," she said, "it's no use talking; we cannot visit upon equal terms with a woman who has mended our collars and sold us anti-macassars. It's too absurd. We've all of us grumbled at her, and told her to call again for her money. Depend upon it she'll remember, and pay us off. She wouldn't be a woman if she did not hate us all round. *I* would if I were in her place. I sha'n't call. I beat her down sixteen pence once over a petticoat body, and I'm sure she'll throw it in my face."

"I never had any dealings with her," pleaded Mrs. Dawkins, "and really considering how dull it is here—"

"Dull?" repeated Lady Louisa. "Did the Bellmontes ever do anything to make it otherwise? Besides, you know, my dear, that little George is four years younger than your youngest."

There was a general titter at this, for good Mrs. Dawkins' matrimonial schemes were well understood.

"Arthur and May would have made it pleasant for our young people," sighed Mrs. Fortescue. "I am so sorry for them."

"You mean you're sorry for yourselves," retorted the outspoken lady of the house.

III. 48

"I am awfully sorry for *my*self. I shall miss them all so much—particularly May— dear little clever thing!"

"I never thought, for my part," Mrs. Dawkins observed, "that she was quite the wife for Arthur, and I'm afraid he'll feel it now."

"I won't hear a word," Lady Louisa gave her table a smart slap with the sugar-tongs, "against May; not a word! I took to her from the first, when she put that purse-proud old Witherspoon down. She sent me a sketch of him as he stood with his mouth wide open taking in the new sensa-tion. It is capital! I'll have it framed and glazed now. *He*'ll call. You may all take your oaths on that, and I hope to heaven he'll marry her (the gentleman was a widower on the look-out), and then I'll forgive him."

Lady Louisa might have been burned for a witch in other days for what was really only worldly wisdom, but might have passed for divination. As the other Lady Bell-monte swept through the lines of bowing servants she thought of other ladies who had sneered at her, and grumbled at her, and told her to call again for four-and-six-pence; and she had, indeed, a rod in pickle for most of them. She held the bewildered boy in her arms, kneeling before him; and her tears—now tender, now angry—blurred the mockery of grief which he wore.

"Don't!" he whimpered petulantly; "don't! you'll spoil my new dress."

"You shall have fifty new dresses—you

darling !" and she clasped him and kissed him till he cried with the pain of those fierce caresses.

"Come," she said at last; "come, and I will show you your grandfather's picture."

She led him to the library, and pointed it out.

"He was your father's father," she explained. "He was Sir George Bellmonte. You are Sir George Bellmonte now. Your father was very like him."

"Was he a thief too ?" asked the boy.

"Hush ! you must not say that. Your father only shot some game—that is not thieving."

"You said he was a thief; you did," persisted her son.

"My child, I was angry. I was very

unhappy in those days, and said things I did not mean. You say things you do not mean when you are in pain. You called me a bad mamma last Sunday, and see! I have got you all this beautiful house."

"Is the picture mine?"

"Everything is yours. Try and understand that you are Sir George Bellmonte of Garcin. You remember the man they used to call Sir Arthur? He had horses and carriages, and fine clothes, and money to buy anything he liked; and now you have everything he had, and can do as he used to do."

"Will he go and live in our house?"

"No, dear, he has gone to London."

"I would like to go to London again; I like London."

"You shall; you have another house there."

"Where we were? You said that was a hotel."

"So it was. Our own house was not ours then, Georgy."

"Why don't you call me Sir George, if I am Sir George?" asked the boy, drawing himself up.

"You darling!" cried the delighted mother. "Every one else shall, but mammas don't call their little boys by their titles. You call me mamma—not Lady Bellmonte."

"You're not Lady Bellmonte!" snapped the boy; "the lady who used to give you work is Lady Bellmonte; you are telling stories, and I hate you." He pushed her

from him, and actually danced and stamped
with sudden rage.

"There, there, calm yourself, my child,"
said his mother; "you will understand it all
when you are older. Don't cry, like a dear
boy, and you shall come and see all the
other pretty things that are yours. If you
are good I will take you to the top of the
house, where there is a beautiful place made
on purpose to look out and see the country
round. I will show you all the fields and
farms that are yours—your very own."

He was taken, well wrapped up, to the
Gazebo, and shown the wide lands of which
he was lord paramount. The pastures
covered with snow like a great sugar-coated
cake; the houses which from that height
and distance he thought were toys taken

out of a box, and dotted here and there; the river running swift and sullen (as rivers will in winter) as though it said to the frost: "Yes, you want to catch and bind me; but you shan't;" all this delighted him, especially the river. He stood up on the balustrade and clapped his hands with glee.

"Why does the river twist and turn like that?" he asked; "why don't it go straight?"

"Rivers never do flow quite straight, dear."

"Does the river belong to me?"

"Well, not entirely. Rivers are something like roads, they belong to every one."

"If it were mine it should go straight— *I'd make it.*" He stamped his foot and cried because it was not his — as other spoiled children have cried for the moon.

It fascinated him as it flowed—here and there all aglow with the red, winter sunset; here and there dark as the coming night; here and there flecked with white foam as it dashed over the *débris* of Castle Hill, and sent a faint murmur far into the keen, clear air. It was no easy task to get him into the house. Once downstairs, he was led from room to room and shown all the pretty things that were his—picture-books, armour, china, curios of all sorts, such as might have taken the fancy of any other child. They gave him only a momentary interest. He fretted for the river, and wanted to be taken back to see it. "My darling!" said his mother, "you have seen it a thousand times."

"It's different," he whined, "up there; I want to go up there."

"You shall to-morrow."

"I want to go now."

"But it is dark."

"I don't care! I want to go—I *will* go." He started off, and flung himself on the floor in a paroxysm of rage when his mother forcibly detained him. He kicked, he roared, he plunged, he scratched, and bit. It was his house, he was master, she (his mother) had told him so, and it was a wicked story. No, it was not. Yes, it was; and if she took his things away from him she was a thief too.

When at last he had sobbed himself to sleep, this Lady Bellmonte sent for the new butler and bade him have a lock fastened on the door which led to the Gazebo immediately, and bring her the key.

Some days after this, Mr. Moule was surprised to receive a summons to wait upon her new ladyship.

"You were a friend of my late husband," she began, "and therefore, I conclude, are not disposed kindly towards me. Nevertheless, I should imagine you will not be above taking a commission from me in the ordinary course of your business, and for which you will be paid."

Mr. Moule did not like this beginning, and he winced slightly at the end of the speech. He did not know what to say, so he bowed. A bow binds so little, and it may be taken to mean so much.

"There is a fragment," her ladyship continued, "which is said to belong to Garcin Abbey."

"It belongs to the Tower," said the little antiquary, *ex cathedrâ.* He was on his own ground now, and confident.

"Have it as you please. I understand it is curiously carved—quite a curiosity in its way. *I* happen to have a taste for such things (with a sneer, as though she would say, ' others had not '), and I wish it to be taken up carefully, Mr. Moule, if you please, and brought here."

Moule bit his lip. "Has your ladyship considered—as one who has a taste for such things—that, taken from its surroundings, it would lose much of the interest which undoubtedly attaches to it ?"

" I have considered everything, sir."

" Including—may I ask ?—the fact, that it is one, the last, of the Sinking Stones of Garcin ? "

" That I have considered most especially. And I will tell you candidly, Mr. Moule, that one of my objects in having it brought here, is to place it on the top of this house, and have it securely fastened there, so as to prevent my boy from being frightened by any old woman's tales."

" Meaning the legend, which had its last fulfilment in your husband's death ? "

" I did not send for you, Mr. Moule, to submit to questioning, but simply to give an order. Will you, or will you not, execute it ? "

" I will not," he replied. " I beg your

ladyship's pardon if I reply too categorically
to your question, but I will take no hand in
what I consider a—never mind what. I
respectfully decline."

"Then I will employ some one else."

"Take care! That fragment is more than
half buried already. The moss covers it
almost entirely. It would ruin it—absolutely ruin it—as a specimen, to have it
tampered with by a mere labourer. And
beside," he added, in a lower tone, "it is on
the very verge of the rift. *It might fall,
Lady Bellmonte.*"

"One excellent reason—from your point
of view—for having it deposited in a safe
place. I think that will do, Mr. Moule."

"Your ladyship is determined?"

"Quite determined."

Poor old Moule was distressed beyond measure. He loathed the idea of having the precious relic, about which he had thought so much, and written so learnedly, touched with rough hands, rooted up as though it were some vulgar paving-stone, and perhaps —horror!—scraped with a spade to clean it. To have it mauled about by masons, a hole drilled through it, perhaps, and impaled on a spike, like a suicide. If by relenting he could be allowed to have his own way about its disposal, get it placed on a pedestal in the centre of the great library, under a glass case, just as it was, with his pamphlet, handsomely bound, laid conveniently near, so that visitors might inform themselves about it — that would be a saving compromise.

"If your ladyship is determined—" he began.

"There is no 'if.' I am."

"Then, under all the circumstances, I would not object to superintend if—oh, l must really protest against the idea of placing it on the roof! In the library now—" And he stated his plan.

Lady Bellmonte heard him out, and was pleased to agree with him. "I am quite open to suggestions as to matters of detail, Mr. Moule, and bow to your superior knowledge as an antiquary; but am quite determined as to the main point. That fragment comes here to the Hall."

"What an ugly thing!" said Sir George, when he first beheld the gargoyle, mounted

as Moule had advised. And to the unæs-
thetic mind he was right. It had immense
ears, no nose to speak of, and its mouth was
a spout. There was an uncanny glare in its
eyes, all stony as they were, which frightened
the boy, but fascinated him.

"I don't like it," he said. "Why does it
keep its mouth open, and stare at me so? Is
it alive? I'm afraid of it."

"My darling! how foolish! It is only a
piece of masonry, very old and curious. It
could not hurt you."

He went closer, and partly satisfied himself. "I want to have it out," he said.

"No, my love. You can look at it as
much as you like, but it is not to be handled.
It is very valuable. Come," said his mother,
taking him by the hand, to lead him away,

III. 49

for as he stood half in wonder and half in fear, it struck her for one instant that the eyes of the gargoyle were like his eyes, and the thought made her shudder.

"I won't come away. It's mine, and I want it."

"Georgy, be good. You don't know how heavy it is. Two strong men could hardly lift it. It is not a plaything."

"It is mine."

"Well, yes, it's yours, but—"

"Then I will have it." So saying, he lifted the trap-bat which he had in his hand, and smashed in one side of the glass case.

CHAPTER VII.

UNWARRANTABLE INTERFERENCE.

THE Bellmontes had been about a week in London when Mr. Drummond wrote the following letter.

"*Temple, Dec.* 19*th.*

" MY DEAR ARTHUR,

"Several letters which I have written to my wife remaining unanswered, I called to-day at your lodgings and was pointedly refused admission. Were it not for the regard I bear you, and the sympathy I feel for your sad reverse of fortune, which, believe me, no one regrets more deeply

than I, I might feel myself justified in
making a more serious protest against what
I cannot but regard as an unwarrantable
interference between husband and wife. I
know that Mrs. Drummond went to Garcin
after her foolish and uncalled-for journey
to the North; that she returned with you
to London; and that she is now staying
under your care. By *you*, I of course mean
you and her cousin; and I have reason to
believe that in neglecting to answer my
letters, and refusing to see me, she is acting
under your, or one of your, advice. This
is certainly wrong, and I might with pro-
priety, if I only considered my own sense
of self-respect, take measures which would
be disagreeable to you, to set it right. But
I will make one last effort to avoid all

unpleasantness, though it is not, perhaps, what I would advise another man in my position to do.

"We have made a lamentable mistake, through no fault of mine. I had undertaken to do you a service at great personal inconvenience and at the risk of estranging the regard which my uncle, your late father, did me the honour to evince for me. By a mere chance I was made aware that my long and faithful attachment to Miss Cowper was reciprocated ; and at a time when I was not quite master of my own actions I asked her to take advantage of a mistake which the people of the house, where we went after the accident, had fallen into, and be really my wife according to the well-established law of Scotland. This I admit

was unwise, but you know—no one better—
what risks a man who is deeply in love
will run.   Have you, my dear Arthur, been
always calculating and prudent either for
yourself or the lady who is now your wife ?
Answer this before you judge me harshly.

" I gave Miss Cowper till the next day to
consider my proposition, wishing that she
might reflect with worldly deliberation, but
hoping—I tell you candidly—that she would
act according to the dictates of her heart.
Before an hour had passed your wife informed me, at her request, that she had
consented.   Now am I not entitled to
presume that that reply was made at Mrs.
Bellmonte's persuasion ?   A delicately-
minded woman like my wife would never
have thus anticipated the time given to her

for replying to such a proposition, unless she had been persuaded; and if a relation and life-long friend who had no interest in the matter but what was for the advised party's good, could make such a recommend-ation—was I, a man deeply in love, to be blamed for acting as I did, and joyfully accepting it?

"Of course I supposed that the ceremony was binding. Any question on that point would be an insult which I could not endure. Let us pass on. I am to blame for not making our union known to my father, my family, and friends. I acted for what I thought was the best, but, I repeat, I was to blame. I gave reasons which (at the time they were given) were cogent, for not going through another form of marriage.

If the first had been valid—as I concluded
it was — a second would have seriously
compromised us. A child will be born to
us before very long, and his whole life
might have been blighted in a way too
obvious to mention, if I had consented to
my wife's request. That was what I thought
at the time, and by the circumstances which
then existed in my mind, and not by those
which afterwards turned out to be the true
facts, must I be judged.

"I dare say my wife thinks that I neglected her. She does not recognise the
exigencies of my position. My practice was
in a highly critical position. I had to work
hard. I had to go out into the world to
gain and keep friends who might be useful
to me. You may say that I might have

secured the latter aid best by taking so cultivated a woman out with me, and securing her aid. Let us grant that again I made a mistake—for whom was it committed?

"For myself? I had enough for my simple bachelor wants before I married. I made it for her and her unborn babe.

"She has found out that in the eyes of the law she is not my wife, and she has left me. I do not blame her for this. She has acted like a pure-minded woman, and I respect her for it. But she should have given me a hearing. She should have given me a chance of repairing the mischief I had unwittingly done — when I knew it. She should have said, 'Norman, we are not legally married; the reasons you gave against

another ceremony are now no longer valid;
will you go through it now?' and I
should have answered 'Yes,' with all my
heart.

"I have made every possible allowance
for her, and in the first letter I wrote—and
I wrote it the moment I obtained your
address—I proposed of my own accord to
marry her in any way she desired. More
than this; the very night she went North,
judging from her manner that I had pained
her in the conversation we had before I left
the house, I wrote to her from my chambers
begging her pardon for having treated the
subject more lightly than I found upon
reflection it deserved; reassuring her of my
continued affection; and consenting to her
request that my father should be invited to

the house, and she be formally presented to him as my wife. This letter she did not receive. Mr. Tyrell intercepted it (with others) at her request, and being inadequate, as I felt, to express my full feeling, I requested him to throw it into the fire, and he did so.

"But the others, written much more fully under more perfect comprehension of the case, she *has* received, and they remain unanswered. What am I to think of this? That she no longer loves me, that she takes advantage of a mistake committed by us both, to cast me off and blight my happiness for ever? I will not harbour such a thought. She is, and has been from the first, my wife in the sight of God ; and some man, contrary to the Divine command, has thrust himself between us to part us asunder.

"I have now only to demand—and I do so in the most formal and solemn manner—that I be admitted to an interview with my wife. I will take whatever she has to say from her own lips, and in no other manner.

"I trust that this request will be complied with. If it be not I shall put it in another way.

"I am,

"Yours sincerely,

"NORMAN DRUMMOND."

"To Arthur Bellmonte, Esq."

The author of this elaborate epistle made a draft of it, corrected, revised, approved, and posted it himself. As a literary effort it received his entire approbation, and such was the man's self - complacency that he almost believed it to be honest. It made him out honest; and what he wanted to be, he thought he was. I have heard it said that no man is a thorough liar until he believes in his own lies. If this be so, Mr. Norman Drummond has attained the acme of mendacity.

He then waited impatiently for the answer, unable to give his mind to anything else. It came sooner than he expected.

"Sir Arthur Bellmonte, sir, to see you," said his clerk, giving the old title from force of habit.

"Show him in," was on his master's lip, but Arthur had already entered. Force of habit again. Drummond held out his hand, but his visitor had both of his in his great-coat pockets. He feared force of habit, and thrust them where they were, as he entered.

"No," he said, more in sadness than anger, "we have something to settle before that."

The dark look came over Drummond's face. His admirable epistle had missed fire then. It grew darker still, as Arthur drew out four letters and laid them on the table. They were unopened, and all addressed to Mrs. Drummond.

"Have you received my letter?" he asked.

"I have, and read it. May has read it too, and she's quicker than I am. It is satisfactory as far as it goes, Drummond, but it does not go quite far enough."

"In what—may I ask—do you find it deficient?"

"In this; you don't say when you first became acquainted with my reverse of fortune (as you call it), and the consequent change in poor Sib's prospects."

"Oh, you're there, are you? If I had been writing to another lawyer I should have put that in, but I didn't want to insult a friend—as I took you to be."

"That won't do. I ask you as a man, when did you know that Sib's weakly brother was heir to Garcin?"

"And as a man I'll answer," said Drummond with a warmth that looked genuine. "On the morning that the brief in your case was delivered here, and after the letter to my wife which I mentioned in mine to you,

was written. You are not satisfied? Simins,
I want you; come here."

The clerk entered.

"When did you post my letter to Mrs.
Drummond?"

"Excuse me, sir, if I may look in my
book?"

"D— your book; well get it."

The book was produced.

"Friday morning the 10th, sir."

"When was the brief *re Bellmonte* delivered?"

"Friday morning the 10th, sir."

"Which did you do first—post the letter,
or take the brief?"

"Post the letter, sir. I was coming back
up the stairs when Bogle and Clerk's man
came."

" You may go. Now !" said Drummond defiantly, " what have you to say ? "

" I am very sorry for you, Norman, very."

" Sorry be d—." Mr. Drummond objected to swearing as a rule, but now having to play the injured and indignant innocent, he thought an oath or two would pay. " I want no man's pity. Go on ; ask some more insulting questions. I'm ready."

" They are not intended as insulting. It seemed to me, and to May, very strange that you should change so suddenly."

" I don't care a straw what you and May think. It's not your business, and I will not endure your interference.

" What does my wife say ? Did she send you here to ask that ? "

III.   50

"She did not; I wish she had."

"Then I'm sorry I answered it, that's all. I decline all further discussion with you, Mr. Bellmonte. I stand by what I wrote. Am I to see my wife and deal with *her?*"

"Norman, let me tell you that I, at least, am satisfied with your explanation. Let us shake hands before I answer that last question."

"You refused me your hand," he replied doggedly.

"I offer it now."

"Well then, there. When am I to see her?"

"I am afraid you must not see her."

"Norman, I do believe you love her. I don't see how you could help loving her, and if you could only explain—"

"I can explain; there's no 'if' about it. Take me with you now, and in half an hour—"

"I left her only half an hour ago, and heaven only knows what has happened since."

"She was going to leave you? Oh this is some new subterfuge."

"She was nearly leaving us all, Norman. She was dying."

"Good God!"

"You must hear it like a man, my poor dear old fellow. I have been very hard against you, but I see clearer now. She was taken ill as we came up in the train, and it turned to brain fever, complicated terribly in a manner you may guess. The child is dead, and she does not know it was born. Poor dear Sib! That is the reason why your letters have not been answered. She has been raving about you in her delirium, calling you all the dearest names."

"And you did not send for me! Oh, Arthur!"

"What was the good? you wouldn't have been allowed to see her. She couldn't read your letters. We didn't like to open them. How were we to know you would care; May—"

"Don't talk to me about her," Drummond interrupted angrily; "you let her lead you by the nose, Arthur; you should have played the man and acted for yourself. But we are wasting time; take me to her. If she be delirious it cannot matter. She

will not know me, and no harm can happen
—I *will* see her."

She was a little quieter when they arrived,
but still wandering. "Pull into the shade,
Norman," she murmured.   Poor girl, she
was back at Minsterton, on the river, living
again in fantasy the happiest days of her
sad life.   "Dearest! let me go there under
the willows, the sun burns me.   Pull hard ;
one or two good strokes and we shall be out
of the stream.   Oh how strong you are!
Ah!" he had taken her thin hot hand in
his—"it's so nice here.   So nice !—There!"
she gave a shriek.   "He is dead, he is
killed; oh my darling, and he will never
know—Yes, Mrs. McPhail, his wife, there
is no mistake about that.   My husband,

Mr. Drummond, wishes it to be generally known."

"You hear her," whispered Drummond to May, who stood near.

"She is raving."

"Yes; but such ravings show what has been in her mind when it was clear. If she dies, I will hold you to a heavy reckoning for what you have done."

"I will not argue with you now, Norman," said May; "there will be time enough for that, if—"

"When will the doctor be here again?"

"Very soon. He said he would be back in two hours."

"I must see him. I will have a second opinion—the best in London."

"Do you think we have not taken that?

—for Sib.   If all we had in the world could save her for one hour, oh how willingly we would give all, all for Sib."

He had left it "to soak," and here was the result ! The still beautiful face ablaze with fever, the glorious hair all gone, the loving, tender lips now murmuring his name with every phrase of affection ; now quivering with pain, now moaning in despair. And it was all his work. He could not play the hypocrite in the face of it. He fell on his knees beside the bed and sobbed, and prayed, and cursed himself in his agony. I suppose that even murderers are sorry for the dead when the deed is done. *And the dead know* —as we think ; and that is why we fear them so, when we have wronged them, living. If she died she would know. Know

the hollowness of his excuses, know the
utter selfishness which prompted them.
Oh! how he would fear her if she died! It
was this thought more than any other that
crushed and humbled him. He might gain
over Arthur; perhaps he had. He might
convince May. He might pass before the
world as a man who had made mistakes and
suffered for them, but to the dead—the
dead that loved him—he would live and die
a scoundrel.

CHAPTER VIII.

MR. DRUMMOND AT GARCIN.

SOCIETY was not at all satisfied with the verdict at which it had arrived at Lady Louisa Dunbrogue's " tea " about the " other Bellmontes," and rather vexed with its dictator. The Fanshawes, the Webbs, and the Carruthers, the rector's wife, and the doctor's, with their sons and their daughters, burned to see how the ex-lace-mender would play the Dame; but after the discomfiture of Mrs. Dawkins, none dared say so. They dropped off by twos and threes, and relieved their feelings by com-

ments more or less conflicting upon the
conduct of their late hostess. "As an
Earl's daughter of course she takes pre-
cedence of us all," said Mrs. Webb. "I
don't dispute *that* for a moment; but really,
considering that she does not belong to the
county, and only lives here because it is
cheap, and is an unmarried woman; I *do*
think she takes too much upon herself in
deciding so roundly for us whom we shall
visit, and whom we shall not."

"What she (meaning Lady Louisa)
said," Mrs. Dawkins told the eldest Miss
Carruthers, "is a very good reason why *she*
shouldn't call. The way in which she used
to beat down the poor woman was disgrace-
ful. I happen to know she gave her only
one pound six for that lace fichu which she

raffled afterwards (pretending it didn't suit her) at ten chances, five shillings each."

" Yes ; she won it herself, and she wears it now," said the younger lady.

"Of course I cannot allow myself to be bound by what passed on such a frivolous subject," observed Mrs. Staines the rectoress. "I took no part in the conversation one way or the other. It was nothing to me ; but as a clergyman's wife it is my duty to go and see her. You need not alter your course, you know ; it will not be visiting in *your* sense of the word."

"Stuff and nonsense!" exclaimed Dr. Barwell, when his spouse informed him of the verdict. "I'm a professional man, and cannot afford to lose so good a patient as that cranky brat will be, for your women's squabbles. Call to-morrow, Maria, and leave my card —•— not the shop one, the other."

When Lady Louisa heard of this revolt, she supposed the butcher and the baker had called also—for orders ; and this made the professional ladies very sore. So they stirred up treason against the Dictator, and before long the card-basket at Garcin Hall was full. "You see, my dears," Mrs. Fortescue explained, "if you had all stuck together I would never have gone. The Dawkinses were there twice in five days, and one cannot be absolutely rude."

They found the other Lady Bellmonte very much what they had found Mrs. Cowper—a cold, distant, (apparently) diffi- dent person, and left burning under the lashes which the "cranky brat," her son, inflicted. For when the cards came in, and the visitor was shown to the drawing-room, his mother would take the dear child on her knee and say, "George, my love, Mrs. So-and-So is down-stairs; she is the nice lady who—" Here would follow something quite the reverse of "nice" which the visitor had said or done; or had it said of her that she had said or done, which is much the same. "You owe my mamma money for mending your old stockings, you do! I *know* you do," he reminded one visitor, "for I couldn't have port wine once, when I was ill, because you were stingy and wouldn't pay. We don't want your money now, and I have port wine every day. I've got more money than you have, and wine, and everything. I don't care for you now—do I mamma?"

He would not come "like a dear" and give another lady a sweet kiss, as bidden; for, said he, "You're a spiteful old thing, you are, and beat your children. If you beat me I'll kill you."

As Society called in pairs for purposes of mutual defence (like skirmishers), you may judge how delightful this was notwithstanding the other Lady Bellmonte's "Oh, Georgies," and "that's naughties," which the cranky brat took at their understood value.

The new *régime* had been established three weeks when her ladyship entertained another sort of visitor, who came by ap-

pointment one Sunday, as it was his only
leisure day.

"This is the man who married your sister
Sibyl," she told her boy, "and I do not
want you to speak to him at all."

"I haven't got a sister," he replied;
"it's one of your stories."

"We'll see about that presently," she
said, as she swept down the stair.

"I am not in the habit, Mr. Drummond,"
she began, "of receiving calls on Sunday,
and have yielded solely out of deference to
your representation that your engagements
do not permit you to leave town on any
other day. You will, therefore, no doubt,
excuse my wishing that we may come to
the point as quickly as possible—and keep
to it. It has become worth your while to

announce your marriage, and you have come, I suppose, to inquire what provision I am prepared to make for my daughter."

Mr. Drummond smiled his superior smile, but braced himself up behind it. He saw the sort of woman he had to deal with, and proceeded to bell the cat at once.

"Your daughter and I are not married, madam," he replied still smiling; "we have resided together for several months, but she is not (unfortunately) my wife. May I venture to suggest that in this young gentleman's presence—"

"Georgy, leave the room, dear."

"I sha'n't."

She took him by the wrist and led him out shrieking. Gave him over to his maid (whom he kicked) and then waited awhile in the corridor with her hand tightly pressed on her side. "God! what a scandal," she murmured, "if these women should find it out!"

She walked straight up to where Drummond sat, carelessly turning over the leaves of a photographic album, and said: "You have come here—to tell me—her mother—that?"

He bowed.

"And thus brutally?"

"Excuse me; you expressed a desire that we should come to the point; and if you will do me the favour to recall your first words to me, you must admit that they did not encourage courtesy."

"Very well; we will go on as we began. Sibyl Cow—Bellmonte was taken from my

care when she was a child, against my wish.
She was a little mischief-maker then, and
caused much trouble between me and my
late husband. I never loved, and I could
not trust her; still I would have done my
duty by her, as a mother, if I had been
allowed to do so. I was not allowed. She
was taken from my care, and I am in no
way—in no way whatever—responsible for
what has become of her. She is now your
mistress—go on."

"Ah, there you are mistaken (smiling
still). If she had had the advantage of your
training I do not think that she could have
grown up to be a more high-minded and
pure woman than she was when I found
her !"

"When you *found* her."

"We resided together, as I have said, for several months, believing that we were husband and wife. The moment she discovered the wretched flaw—of which presently—in our marriage, she left me."

The other Lady Bellmonte took her hand from her side, and moved towards a seat. Till now she had stood in front of him, two fingers on the table, and he looked into her face and read it. Moreover, he felt the table tremble. As she turned, he placed a chair for her with his most gentlemanly "Permit me."

"Shall we go on," he resumed, "in this very business-like manner, or may I address you as a mother?"

"I tell you candidly, Mr. Drummond, I do not feel in the least like a mother to Sibyl. She has never given me a chance."

"Then may I speak to you as a woman, of another woman's undeserved sufferings?" His voice sank, his eyes softened. In spite of herself she had to be civil. Besides, there was the scandal—grown a shade or so less black—but still a scandal, to be hushed up somehow. She thought how she could use such a one against those proud Carruthers, and softened.

"I did begin rudely," she replied, with not a bad attempt at frankness. "You put me out, coming—well let us make peace," and she held out her hand.

He raised it respectfully to his lips.

Then he told her the story—his own version of it, you may be sure—throwing in just enough of self-reproach and injured innocence to make it as plausible as possible. How, worried with business, he had answered his poor Sibyl curtly about the validity of their marriage; how he had so considerately written to allay her fears; how she had gone North to satisfy herself, before his well-meant assurances and expressions of regret could reach her; how she had been at death's-door with brain fever; how he had nursed her till her return to consciousness made her liable to be shocked at his presence by her side; and lastly, how he had sought her only surviving parent, to confess and deplore all he had done that was wrong, and pray for aid in setting it right again.

"Then why, in heaven's name," said her

ladyship, "don't you get really married?
Where's the difficulty?"

"I will tell you," he replied, drawing
closer his chair. "When her errand North
was completed she came here."

"Here! impossible."

"It was before your—your time. She
came to her friends and cousins, the Arthur
Bellmontes."

"And never saw me! I heard there
was a lady with them, but never guessed it
could be she. She might have sought her
mother."

"We will let that pass. She was in deep
distress; we must not blame her, dear Lady
Bellmonte, for going to those who were in a
great manner responsible for it. Now I
don't want to say a word against Arthur.

He and I have been friendly for some time, and I believe are so still. *I* am to him. But his wife! You know her."

"None better. Is she not my niece?"

"She governs him completely. He is not a clever man, and is in leading-strings to her. And she has an absurd idea—when I saw your fine boy here just now I quite laughed at it;—she has an idea that I am actuated by mercenary motives—do you follow me?"

"I think I do."

"Nothing could be more ridiculous. Why that young rascal will make you a grand-mother before we know where we are!"

Mothers do not mind their sons being called "young rascals" in that tone, and so this one smiled.

"As a lawyer," Drummond went on, "I know that you have your dower—a handsome provision in the eyes of a poor working-man like me, but a bare sufficiency for the wants of a lady in your position—and which of course is only for your life. So what have I to expect?"

"Nothing," she replied, quickly. "I could not—"

"Wait till I ask." Again the superior smile. Lady Bellmonte was fond of money, and it reassured her.

"Mrs. Arthur cannot, and will not, understand this," Drummond resumed; "and from her manner I feel sure that all her influence will be used against me. The first impulse of a woman of any delicacy (and the impulses of your sex are generally

right), would be to say, Marry him at *any*
risks. Leave him at the church door, if
you doubt him ; but cover up this dreadful
slight upon your character by a legal
marriage."

"I should say so."

"Ah, but you are not May Fairfax."

The other Lady Bellmonte thought awhile,
and an evil look passed over her face.

"She may be counting upon coming back
here," she said.

"Do not let us impute bad motives."

"Bah ! Don't you see that the very
motives she attributes to you operate in her
own case ? If anything—which God forbid,
should happen to my darling boy, and Sibyl
died unmarried, Mrs. Arthur or her children
would come back here."

"I did not think of that," he mused. This was false. He had the base insinuation made up and sharpened for future use.

"Why it is as clear as day! And her husband sees it too. You think Mr. Bellmonte an easy-going man, led by his wife. Let me tell you, sir, that he is no such simpleton. He has tried to injure me as no simpleton could do. He knew more than is generally supposed, or why did he indulge my husband as he did. I would never rest easy in my grave if I thought that that man could ever come back here as master."

"Then you will help me?" His manner told her she had been a little too eager, and she drew back.

"Tell me how."

"Use your influence with my poor Sibyl.

Take her away from the bad counsels of those Bellmontes. Invite her down here when she is well enough to be moved. Change of air and scene will be requisite. It is only natural that she should be with you—her mother. Give me the opportunity of pleading with her unbiassed by false friends. She is my cousin just as much as she is Arthur's; is it likely I would wish to injure a Bellmonte, if only for my dead mother's sake?—and I love her so dearly, and value her good name still more. Give her the opportunity of knowing her best friend — her mother. Restore us to the happiness we once enjoyed. Oh, it would be a noble act; one you would never, never repent."

" But if she should decline."

"She will not decline. She can be easily
made to feel what is the truth; that she is a
burden where she is. They have been put
to heavy expenses for her as it is, and will
not take a penny of mine. Leave this to
me, Lady Bellmonte. Write her two lines
in this sense: '*Let bygones be bygones; come
to your mother*'—and I will answer for the
rest."

"It shall be done. You will stay to
luncheon ?"

"With pleasure. Shall I see my young
cousin ?"

He saw his young cousin, and was permitted to assure him he had a sister, "and
perhaps a brother too," Mr. Drummond
added pleasantly. "How should you like

to have a big brother to play with you?"

"I'd rather have a small one," replied the dear child, "and then I could whip him."

"Little beast!" muttered Drummond to himself. "Fits and bad temper! The one will breed the other, and the two will kill him."

After luncheon, Lady Bellmonte, who was much taken with her visitor's courteous manner, and (apparent) sincerity, broached a subject which had been dwelling on her mind since the episode of the glass case.

"My Georgy is a high-spirited boy," she observed, "and I fear he is getting a little too much for me. I am not as strong as I was, Mr. Drummond, and have been think-

ing I ought to get him a tutor.   Boys are
all the better for a man's authority over
them—don't you think so ?   Georgy really
requires a firm, judicious hand over him.
Do you know of any person who would
be likely to suit ? "

"At this moment, no ; however, I will
inquire.   Tutors are plentiful enough, but
what you want is rather rare.   In the first
place,"—Mr. Norman Drummond assumed
his judicial air, and ticked off the heads on
his fingers—" you must have a gentleman.
Scholarship may be put aside just now.
The man must be before all things a gentleman ; as a quick boy like yours would soon
pick up bad manners.   Then he must be
cheerful and sympathetic, lead George to
acquire a taste for manly sports, and join in

them with him.   He must be, as you say,
judiciously firm—not severe."

"Oh no," chimed in the fond mother;
"not severe."

"And his appearance and manners must
be such as to inspire respect.   Many a com-
petent and estimable person has failed to
get on with his pupils because they have
heard him lightly spoken of as 'only the
tutor,' or some such disparaging phrase as
that.   Sir George Bellmonte's tutor ought
to be able to hold his own with any gentleman, old or young, who may visit this house.
Lastly—and this is directed to yourself—if
such a man presented himself, money should
be no object, on your side.   He should be
worth—let me see—at least two hundred a
year."

At this she winced.

"So much."

"My dear Lady Bellmonte, believe me that it is easier to select an excellent bishop than to find a passably good tutor for an only son. I will bear what you want in mind, and let you know. But you must give me time, for I shall not make a hasty recommendation. You may depend upon that."

The following Monday night he went into the back slums and there he found his man —a man who had worn Her Majesty's scarlet, who had simpered in gilded salons, for whom bright eyes had grown brighter, and many a bitter tear had been shed—a man who had flung most gifts of birth and educa-

tion into the gutter, and had drowned ac-
quirements of no mean order, first of all in
champagne, and latterly in gin. Mr. Drummond found him making political speeches
in the bar-room of a low public-house for
his board and drink. The board did not
cost his patron much, but the drinks mounted
up to a pretty penny on Saturday night.
Still he paid; for he drew customers, and
they had liquors drawn for him.

Drummond called him out into the street,
and had a good look at him under a gas-
lamp. Still handsome, still the voice and
bearing of a gentleman, very reckless, and
exceedingly seedy.

" How many chances have you had,
Dashwood," he asked, " of getting out of
this ? "

"About six," the other replied, with indifference.

"If I gave you another, what would you do with it?"

"Send it after the rest, I dare say. What is it?"

"Bear-leading."

"I've been there," Dashwood replied, with a scoff; "young hopeful learned too much; but I don't mind trying again if the people are not cads. Who are they?"

"We can't talk here. Come to my chambers to-morrow as soon after ten as you are quite sober; will you?—and I'll tell you all about it."

He assented, and Drummond left him, musing, "If he will behave himself for a month or six weeks, and then get drunk at the right time, so that the little beast tumbles into the river or breaks his neck, it will be all right."

CHAPTER IX.

ON NE BADINE PAS AVEC L'AMOUR.

" NORMAN, dearest ! where is Norman ? " were almost the first words murmured by our Sib when her magnificent constitution dragged her from the very jaws of death. She was told that he had been constantly at her side up to that hour, when the doctor's decree banished him for awhile. She was to see no one but the nurse and May, and not to speak to them, or they too would be sent out of the room. She had only to be quiet to get well. Thus the great medico in his confident, quiet way, which to convalescents was better than all the drugs in the pharmacopœia.

As she gained strength, May found that her memory as to the recent past was failing her. She spoke of Drummond as her dear husband, wanted to know why she was not in her own house, and oh, how kind they (the Bellmontes) were to come from Garcin to nurse her! Dear Norman would be going circuit again soon; would they mind taking her back with them?—the country air, she thought, would do her good, and she would be quite well and strong again by the time he came back.

Under these circumstances Mr. Drummond (who by this time was permitted to see her for short spells) had to modify his plans. It would not do to deliver the other Lady

Bellmonte's letter just yet.   If this absence
of memory continued, it would make plane
(why will people write it *plain?*) sailing for
him, if that cursed little meddling fool
(meaning Arthur) were out of the way.   He
might take Sib back with him to Chelsea,
remind her cautiously of what they had said
about his father's prejudices, marry her, and
turn over a new leaf.   Yes; the new leaf
should certainly be turned.   Setting aside
ulterior prospects, the only sister of Sir
George Bellmonte of Garcin Hall was a
widely different person from the daughter of
a convicted poacher and a woman who
mended lace for a living.

He did not misjudge or over-estimate
May's opposition.   With a woman's quick-
ness she suspected the security of this

change of front; and woman-like she would not let him imagine that he was deceiving her. This, my dear Madam, is one of the few mistakes which your charming sex habitually commit. When a lord of the creation sets a trap for you, you sing out: *"It's a trap! I see it! come, dears, and look at the trap!"* You should pretend not to know it's a trap, hop playfully round and round it, and over it, and on it, letting him think that the next hop will be *in* it; or else, being a brute, he'll out with his gun, slip in a No. 4 cartridge, and pop!—over you go. This requires a good deal of self-denial; it is so hateful, I own, to be clever and not show it; but, believe me, your sacrifice will be rewarded.

May had had her lesson. She remembered how the happiness of her life was dimmed by the shadow of deceit. She felt how delightful it was now to look her husband in the face and know that nothing could spring into light to diminish his love. He had long ceased to doubt whether it was happiness or misery which her frank confession had brought upon him. Sib should be dealt with as she had treated Arthur. All the doors and windows (so to speak) of her life should be flung open. The sunshine and the keen breezes of truth should enter. Every loathsome crawling reptile that had lurked in the once dark corners should be crushed; any unwholesome vapour should be blown away; and love should find a temple swept and garnished to abide in.

Utopian, of course. What man ever did

sweep out his life to let a woman in ? There
are some things he will burn, and some he
will cover up, and some he will lock away
in the little cupboard whereof he keeps the
key ; but a clean sweep ?—never !

So far May's views—if they erred at all—
erred in a right direction. She had others
against which all the proprieties would cry,
" Shocking ! "—and we all know that when
the proprieties confess themselves shocked,
there is no more to be said. Brought up as
she had been to think for herself upon sub-
jects deeply affecting the happiness of her
sex, she could not understand how a man
who was a scoundrel, and had treated a
woman like a scoundrel, made her reparation
by getting a legal right to continue the
process. If Mr. Drummond were as she

supposed him to be, then poor, dear, innocent, ill-used Sib was exceedingly well rid
of him. She scoffed the parting at the
church-door idea, which she had been told
(through Arthur) every pure-minded woman
ought to entertain. " What ! tie herself for
life to a brute, and give up all hope of being
happy with a better man—how utterly absurd ! Never be able to marry with this
cloud over her ? There is *no* cloud over her.
If I were a man I'd marry her to-morrow—
the darling ! "

To sum up. If Mr. Drummond could
explain away his (apparently) bad conduct,
or if he confessed all like a man (or rather
*un*like a man ; for a man never does confess
all), and Sib would forgive him, then May
would go to their wedding ; but if there

was to be a half-and-half explanation, and sham confessions, and twaddle about *reparation;* " then," said the sturdy little woman, " Sib is better, and likely to be happier, as she is, than she would be as his wife."

May was in this frame of mind when Mr. Norman Drummond's plan for taking advantage of Sib's bad memory was broached; and " Now," cried May in triumph, "*now I know* he is a villain."

Hitherto Lady Bellmonte (for so Arthur's mother continued to be called, as nothing on earth could make her drop the title she had borne so long and so well) had gone against her daughter-in-law in these disputes; not sharing May's enthusiasm for Sib; and being influenced by the regard which Sir Alexander had entertained, and his son still felt, for Drummond. But this proposition, all cunningly put forward as it was, shook their belief in the gentleman, and rooted May's prejudice as firm as Chimborazo.

In the mean while, Arthur Bellmonte had found Mr. Drummond only too correct in one particular, namely, his estimate of difficulties attending the finding of something to do for a living. His wife had secured to herself four hundred a year, which the other Lady Bellmonte, hungering after *mesne profits* partly out of spite, and partly out of greed, could not touch. But this the loyal girl had made over to her husband's mother, with his full consent. It had been Sir Alexander's private fortune, quite apart from Garcin; it was morally his widow's, and they made it so in law. They would live with her till Arthur found something to do—that was all. And they had six out of that eight hundred pounds wind-fall (or rather, lease-fall), into which May had come at her marriage. Quite a little fortune, thought this happy, hopeful pair, and they insisted upon paying their share of the housekeeping out of it.

They had six hundred pounds to begin with, but Sib's illness cost them nearly a hundred in doctors' fees alone, and their capital was further reduced by an unfortunate operation into which Arthur was led soon after he arrived in town. THE READY RELIEF ASSOCIATION (*Limited*), addressing itself to Retired Officers and others, advertised for a secretary, who was to deposit three hundred pounds as security for the proper discharge of his delicate and responsible duties, and his salary was to be five hundred a year. The R. R. A. had its chambers—it scorned the word " office "—near St. James's Street, where it was established for the purpose of assisting noblemen and gentlemen out of those temporary difficulties in which the fashionable world is sometimes placed, by loans upon personal security to be made without the harassing formalities which money-lenders impose, and upon the most reasonable terms. The chambers consisted of a reception-room, where noblemen and gentlemen found another sort of temporary relief in " Pollie and B.," sherry, cigars, and other creature comforts ; the Secretary's sanctum—a perfect gem of decorative art—

and the Board-room, a more demure apart-
ment, where the directors met on Tuesdays,
and advanced funds on purely philanthropic
principles. Arthur was one of thirty-six
candidates, and to his great joy was selected
for the post. "You see," said the managing
director, "all our dealings are with gentlemen, we want them treated with like gentlemen; and your inexperience of business
habits (which is only another phrase for
business slang), instead of being a drawback,
is actually a recommendation." So he
deposited his (or rather May's) three hundred pounds, and was exactly four days in
office when he found that the Association
consisted of one Mr. Beecker Moss, a bank-
rupt usurer of the lowest type, who had run
off with his money (and left a good many

others in the lurch) the very day it was paid.

He then found that the very reverse of the Beecker Moss dictum prevailed. Ignorance of business habits (in other words, the knack of doing the right thing in the right way) was a drawback, and not a recommendation. His father—leading the retired life we have seen—had dropped his old friends. The son had made none in his prosperity who could help him now.

" Awfully sorry, old fellow, you know. All ours were cut up like the deuce when we heard it. Go in for a government appointment, if I were you," came from young fellows of his own standing, and his old habits.

Go in for a government appointment!

Easier said than done now-a-days. He was too old to enter the civil service by its front door, for the back ones he had no "open sesame." In one month's weary seeking, half his capital had vanished, and nearly all his hope.

These disappointments could not be kept from Sib, and well-directed hints from Mr. Drummond made her chafe under the reflection that she was a burden upon May's shrunken means.

"At all events," she said one day, "you can come and live with me when I can get out. I shall always consider the house you gave me as yours, and there will be plenty of room for us all."

Now as "us all" from her lips just then, included Mr. Norman Drummond, May thought this a good opportunity for getting at how much Sib remembered of the past. She found that a good deal of it had come back, doubtless at Drummond's bidding (for he saw her now every day), and consequently, if this were so, you may be sure that the best face was put upon it.

" What an unlucky old darling you are!" May began. " First you get nearly killed in a railway smash, and then you all but die of brain fever, and when you came to us for the first time in your distress, we had no home to offer you."

" Not one of your own, dearest; but oh! how good you have been to me in it!"

" Don't you remember coming to Garcin?"

" I never was at Garcin."

" Not when you came from Scotland?"

"Why we went straight to the Charing Cross Hotel."

"Yes, but when you came back alone, the second time?"

"The *second* time?"

"Tell me all you can remember that has happened since. Well, you had a quarrel with Norman at your own house. You recollect that?"

"Yes. I was very foolish. Don't let us talk of that."

"Has he told you, you were foolish?"

"No, dear fellow! he takes all the blame on himself."

"He treated you shamefully," May broke in warmly, upset by the "dear fellow"— "neglected you—threw doubts on the legality of your marriage."

"So I thought, and it pained me horribly,
I fainted when he left, and I don't know
much about what happened afterwards, till
I found myself here. But May, my pet,
you are a wife too, now; and your dear
Arthur has his troubles and anxieties.
Men cannot be lovers all their lives. They
have a thousand things to worry them that
we don't know of. You wouldn't blame
Arthur for not being always as he was."

The comparison put May's face in a blaze,
and words were on her lips which afterwards
she was glad not to have spoken.

"From something he has said," Sib resumed, "I am afraid that I have not been
to him all that a wife—no, he did not say so.
I guessed it from his tone. He is not a
demonstrative man, you know, but his feel-

ings are deep and sensitive. I was afraid of
showing him how much, and how deeply, I
loved him. I think he got to feel that I
didn't care about his being so much away,
and all this time I was starving for the
sound of his voice. I know him better
now," she said, with her sweet, sad smile.
" We shall know each other better."

" Then let him tell you everything."

" He has, dear."

" He has *not*. Will you let me read you
a letter he wrote to Arthur ? "

" About us ? "

" Yes."

" I would rather he told me himself,
dear."

" He never will, unless you ask him point-
blank."

" I have nothing to ask him."

" You have. You ought to read that letter, Sib," May persisted, a bright thought striking her, " He wrote it in self-defence."

" Oh, then I will."

So the elaborate epistle was read, and naturally gave rise to much questioning. Sib found she had by no means been told everything, and the lapse of memory thus disclosed frightened her. " He did it for the best, I'm sure," she said after a while. " I'm sure of that, and yet—I'm glad you showed me the letter. May, what a complete exoneration it is. And how beautifully expressed."

" Oh, beautifully ! Reads like a book," said May drily.

"It was so good of him to write to me that night. Oh, why didn't I wait?"

"You say you fainted when he left you. Why didn't he stay and take care of you?"

"He had gone when I fell."

"How long?"

"Oh, I cannot say. When I heard the door close behind him, it sounded like the crash of something that crushed me. I was out of my mind, or I would never have done as I did."

"Did he not kiss you at parting?"

"I—I don't think he did."

"And he left you just about to faint, having said things which maddened you, without a kiss, or a good-bye, or anything . to comfort you?"

"I suppose he was vexed. I dare say

I put on that nasty cold manner I have, and said cutting things; but remember, dear, the moment he got to his chambers he wrote to comfort me."

"Do you know," May asked pointedly, "that our misfortunes were made public that day? The clubs were ringing with it."

"Well, dear—what then? He did not know. I think we began by talking about you. I said that very likely you would invite me to Garcin the next time he went circuit; and he made no remark."

"Sib," said May, in a tone more serious than her words, "you might go to heaven and teach the angels to be good and true, but a child knows more than you do of this world's guile. Don't you think that our misfortunes make you a very different sort of wife for a man like Norman Drummond than you were? You seem to forget that you are a Bellmonte, and Arthur's and Norman's cousin as well as mine." Your brother isn't likely to live long, and when he dies you will be mistress of Garcin."

Sib had never realized this. Her separation from her mother was so early in her life, and so complete, that until now she had not associated herself in any way with the change of fortune which had advanced the brother she had never seen, and the mother whom time and neglect had made a stranger to her. May's words came upon her like an accusation.

"I could not help it, dear," she said, as though pleading for her own fault.

"Of course you could not help it. Who said you could? The position is made for you, and is yours whether you like it or no. The point is, Did Norman know of it when he wrote that letter? It's nonsense to suppose that a man who had neglected you for months, had refused your requests to your face, and left you as he did; should turn round all of a sudden, and be so considerate and yielding without some motive. I can understand a man yielding to his wife's face, and taking it back in a letter when he got to his chambers, but not the reverse. Men don't get soft in their chambers, Sib; they are cocks of the walk there. That's the place to write a nasty letter from—not a nice one."

"But we know that this *was* a nice one.

See (taking up the elaborate epistle and reading) :

"*I wrote to her from my chambers begging her pardon for having treated the subject more lightly than I found upon reflection that it deserved; reassuring her of my continued affection, and consenting to her request that my father should be invited to the house and be formally presented to her as my wife.*"

"That's what he wrote."

"What he *says* he wrote," May persisted. "I should so like to have seen it. If I had been in his place (and was honest), I would never have burned it."

"1 dare say he is sorry that he did so now," Sib replied. "He did not think of the injurious doubts which would be thrown upon so trivial an act."

"That's how you used to speak to Uncle Tom." May had a catch in her throat, and (to her) a strange sensation of fright. "You never spoke to me before in such a tone."

"I am speaking for my husband."

"Oh, Sib, don't—*don't* look at me so," cried May. She fell on her knees, her arms wound about Sib's waist; her face was hidden in her dress in the old childish way; but there was all a sorrowful woman's depth of pleading in her voice. "I cannot bear it. I doubt him because I love you. Oh, Sib, you know I love you. Put your hand on my head as you used to do when I was naughty, and begged pardon. No—I don't beg pardon now," she added quickly. "I only want to be sure you believe I love you in all I say and in all I think. Why, what motive can I possibly have?"

"May I be allowed to suggest one?" replied a voice from the door at which Mr. Norman Drummond had been standing for some time, unperceived. May felt as though she had been stabbed to the heart when Sib wrestled herself free, tottered towards this man, and was caught sobbing in his arms.

"If I may suggest one," Drummond resumed, caressing the beautiful head which dropped on his shoulder, " it would be this. If Sir George does not live, and this lady's mind be turned against me, you and your husband would have good prospects of regaining Garcin, Mrs. Bellmonte. Stay; that is hardly fair. I should leave him out.

Arthur's an honourable man. You might slip on the ruins of your cousin's life up to the position you schemed so nicely to gain."

She was not only stabbed now, the knife had been turned in the wound.

"Sib," she gasped, "Sib, darling! do you believe that such a thought ever entered my mind? Don't you see he must be false to harbour such a— oh, Sib, look at me."

He pressed the face which is turning at this appeal back to its place on his breast. "Do not excite yourself, my love," he said. "I will answer for you. If there be falsehood in the suspicion, Mrs. Bellmonte, you must excuse my asking in whose mind it originated. The responsibility for our hasty marriage is almost entirely yours. When Garcin was, as you thought, in your grasp;

when it suited you to conceal an escapade
which it was not convenient for the future
Lady Bellmonte to have talked about; you
were delighted to give me your cousin.
You made us a valuable wedding present;
nothing was too good for us. You gushed
over the prospect of our being blessed with
an heir—to-nothing. Now when a mistake
has been discovered, which to a woman can
but have one remedy, you come between us.
You take advantage of this poor trembling
creature's weakness to sow doubt and hatred
in her heart. For shame, for shame! Don't
cry, dearest, there must be an end to this.
You have asked for your motive (this to
May), and I have told you. Beware of
two-edged swords, Mrs. Bellmonte—they are
awkward weapons."

"I cannot answer him, Sib," May replied. She was pale as death and trembling all over. "I know he is wicked and false to the core. I see it in his face, but I cannot, I will not, answer him. How dare he say such things of me! And you cling to him, Sib; you let him kiss you."

"He is my husband. He loves me."

"He loves Garcin," said May bitterly.

"My best beloved,"—Drummond spoke with that low tender voice which first thrilled her heart—"let us end this. Will you ask me if I went straight to my chambers that night?"

"To satisfy her, dear Norman. Her affection for me blinds her. You must not be angry with poor May."

"Be it so. To satisfy Mrs. Bellmonte,

then, I say that I went straight to my chambers, and did not speak to a soul on the way. There might have been any amount of chatter at the clubs; I did not go near mine. Now this is to you, Sib. Upon my honour as a man—by the love I hope to have restored between us, I swear to you that when I wrote that letter I had no more idea of your ever having Garcin than of your ever having the moon. Is that enough?"

"Oh, May, you must believe him now!"

"It is not necessary that she should," Drummond observed haughtily. "I have said all I intend to say—except this. Our ideas are so widely apart, and further discussions upon them are likely to be so detrimental to you, my love, that I think

III.   54

you had better return to your own home."

" He is afraid of me, Sib—mark that," cried May.

"Quite so," replied Drummond, calmly. "As I should be of a draught, or a d— excuse me, I was going to say something unpolite—or anything which in her present delicate state of health might harm or shock Sibyl."

" Oh, if I could only be a man for one half-hour!" exclaimed May.

"I should be much less afraid of you then, Mrs. Bellmonte; one knows how to deal with a man; but an angry, unreasonable woman has advantages with which I really cannot attempt to cope," said Drummond. " A retreat is one's only resource. Do you not think (this to Sib) that you are strong enough to move to-day ? "

" No, she is not," May answered for her.

" And I am afraid I must insist upon breaking up another little project," Drummond went on, not heeding the interruption. " When you do return to your own house I hope you will be satisfied with my company there."

" He means to part us, oh, Sib ! to—he means more than that; I actually believe he is base enough to fancy I want to go there, to live upon you. Is that what you mean, Mr. Drummond ? "

" It is enough for me to say that I wish to have my wife to myself."

" She is not your wife."

" Sibyl, my dearest, if I get a special

license will you marry me to-morrow, at
your own house ?"

"No Sib, no! tell him *no*," May pleaded
in an agony of love and fear. "Give me a
few days to think—a week. You are not
well enough; it would kill you. If we part
like this it would break my heart. And I
might think better of it, Sib. I might if I
had only time to think, and I would beg his
pardon if I found I was wrong. Oh, Sib,
after all these years don't let us part like
this ! "

"You will have to choose between us,"
whispered Drummond in her ear.

May was on her knees again, but the pale
eager face was not hidden.

" Sib," she cried again. " Mother, sister,
dearest, best, truest friend, say NO ! Give

me ten days; only ten short days. I won't breathe a word against him. I wont mention his name. I'll talk it over with Arthur and Lady Bellmonte—not with you at all. I will try to believe in him for your sake. I'll try to like him again. I will do anything, bear anything, except to part with you like this."

"You will have to choose between us;" Mr. Drummond repeated this aloud now— and made a mistake.

"That is harsh," Sib said, withdrawing herself from his embrace, and lifting poor weeping May; "too harsh, Norman; when you see how she loves me. It shall be as you wish, dearest—there! don't cry. We will be married in ten days; that is quite soon enough."

CHAPTER X.

THE BONFIRE.

MR. DASHWOOD was installed at Garcin Hall as tutor to the young baronet, and gave universal satisfaction. To account for this phenomenon we must be present at a scene which took place in the bath-room on the fourth morning of the new *régime*.

Sir George had been ordered cold sea-water baths, the raw material for which was brought up daily from the coast in casks, and was afterwards thrown away much as it came; for this reason. The dear boy disapproved of cold water, and so maltreated the wretched woman whose duty it was to preside over his ablutions, that she gladly became a party to a deception under which the dear boy was to be represented as much too brave to require supervision, and was to make a great splashing (with his sponge) so as to lead his fond mother to suppose he was quite enjoying himself in his bath. Whilst performing this little farce on the morning in question with nothing on him but his night-gown, there entered "to him," as the old dramatists would have it, Mr. Dashwood, who, placing his right foot on a chair, stripped up the leg of the trouser, and disclosed a red and black streak about three inches long on the bared skin.

"Do you see that, you little devil?" he

demanded with somewhat of the judicious firmness required of him.

"It's where I kicked you last night," replied the boy with a satisfied grin; "and I'll tell Ma you called me a devil."

Before he could guess what was to happen, Mr. Dashwood took him carefully by the throat with one hand, and by the left ancle with the other; plunged him backwards in the bath, and held him under water—head and all—for fifteen seconds, well measured.

As soon as the patient had disposed of about a breakfast-cup full of salt water which he had taken during the immersion, he rushed towards the door, and just got out a gasp of " Ma!" when he was seized again in the same manner, and held under water for twenty seconds.

. "Now then," said Dashwood, "I don't think you will call 'Ma!' again — will you?"

The victim was now thoroughly cowed. He lay on the floor shivering with cold and terror, and could not call for help even if he had dared to do so.

"You haven't a mark on you to show that you've been punished," said his tutor; "and as I can prove you to be a little liar about your bath, you wouldn't be believed against me if you were to tell what I've done to you. But if you *do* tell any one, do you know what I'll do? I'll take you down to the river where it's black and deep, and I'll hold you under for two hours—do you understand?"

"Ye—es."

"Very well. Take off that wet gown and dry yourself (tossing him a towel); you have fits, don't you? Do you like them?"

"N—o—o."

"Ah, now look here." As he spoke, the judicious tutor took up the soap and swallowed it; took up the bath-brush and swallowed that also; drew off one of his boots, shook it upside down in the air, and then produced two white mice out of it! Any fifth-rate conjurer could have done better, but Sir George Bellmonte had never seen any conjuring at all, and stood aghast at the marvels presented.

"I'm not a man," Dashwood explained, leisurely putting on his boot; "I'm a Genii. You dare to kick me again, or to say *no* when I say yes, or *yes* when I say no; and you shall have a fit every half-hour for the rest of your life. How would you like that?"

The dear boy had heard of Genii, and it dawned upon him that this one, properly handled, might be useful.

"Have you got a lamp?" he asked all of a tremble.

"Lots; and rings, and carpets that will fly, and every sort of Genii business. Now look here again. Do what I tell you. Hold your tongue about what I do, unless I give you leave to speak, and there is no end to the nice things you shall have. You shall have those pretty white mice to begin with, and I'll get you a cage for them. Disobey me once, and you shall go under the river for two hours, and have twenty-four fits a day—which shall it be ?"

" I'll—I'll be good. Why do the mice have such funny red tails ?"

" They're not really mice. They are two kings I changed to mice because they told stories about me. I had a great mind just now to change you into a water - rat," he added severely. The boy was afraid of rats and hated water; so the combination was sufficiently horrid.

" Oh, please don't !" he cried. " I wont tell."

" You'd better not ; now throw your wet shirt into the bath and come downstairs."

"I went up this morning to see Sir George take his bath," the judicious one told Lady Bellmonte at breakfast, "and upon my word *I* could not have plunged in as pluckily as he did on such a cold morning."

"Dear boy," replied the pleased mother; "I don't think he knows what fear is."

The dear boy caught his tutor's eye, and declared he was not afraid of anything.

Thus it was that Dashwood gave entire satisfaction.

"So nice and judicious," Lady Bellmonte told Mrs. Dawkins. "Treats him as though they were both boys, and at the same time has a control over him, such as I really did not expect any one could obtain with so high-spirited a child."

So you may conclude he got his *quid* for his *quo*.

"I say," he asked Dashwood one day;
"does Ma know you're a Genii?"

"Women don't understand these things,"
the enchanter replied loftily; "or common
people either—I'm only a Genii for Kings
and Baronets."

This pleased the boy. "Well," he said,
"I'm a Baronet."

"That's so," his tutor observed, as though
the thought had only just struck him.

"So as you're a Genii for me," the boy
resumed, "and can change things, won't you
change something I want you to?"

"What is it?"

"A nasty ugly stone thing in the library;
I want you to change it into a cat, and get
me a gun and let me shoot it."

"What for?"

" I don't like it—I'm afraid of it—it lays on its back and stares at me wherever I am. Do please make it a cat. I killed a cat once in the stable with a pitch-fork, and it was such fun."

Now Mr. Dashwood, in his capacity as a Genii, had already converted a pair of gloves into an orange, and had produced sparrows out of a ginger-beer bottle, to the increased wonder and delight of his pupil, but the last of the Sinking Stones was a trifle too heavy for such legerdemain, and so he had to procrastinate.

" This isn't good weather for changing stones," he explained gravely. " When they are changed in the winter to cats, the Snarks sometimes come after them. Do you know what a Snark is ? " And being answered in the negative, he read out part of a quaint piece of nonsense written by the best friend children have had for many a year. This caused a diversion for the time, but day after day the boy returned to his half-crazy desire. "When would Snarks be out of season?" he would ask over and over again.

One day Dashwood being hard pressed on this point, he remarked, "It's too much trouble to turn it into a cat and kill it. I'll tell you what we'll do. Next Guy Fawkes day we'll have a bonfire and burn it up."

"But stones won't burn."

"That sort of stone burns beautifully," said Dashwood; "all red and blue fire," and he thought he had disposed of his difficulty, as no further questions were asked.

Not much learning did the heir of Garcin gain under this Mentor, but many unlawful tastes did he acquire, and many dreadful things did he do—all on the sly. He smoked cigarettes, he drank rum-shrub, he was taught to use a light gun and shoot things. He was taken into the town, and treated to tarts and toffy, delicacies which all the Faculty had strictly forbidden. He became quite fond of his tutor, obeyed him implicitly, called him "dear Mr. Dashwood!" and asked questions in the Sandford and Merton tone, to his mother's intense delight. The new tutor was the very pink and pearl of pedagogues, and how clever it was of Mr. Drummond to select so good a man!

"Ma," said her son once when they were alone. "What is Guy Fawkes?"

He was given a short (and wholly incorrect) biography of that ·distinguished traitor, and then he asked, "Do they *burn* him because they hate him." He was told that it was wicked to hate even sinners, but proper to evince reprobation of their sin. This, however, was not satisfying. "They don't burn his sin," he remarked; "they burn *him*."

"You silly child," laughed his mother, "he has been dead for more years than you can count. They only burn a *stuffed figure* with an ugly mask on."

"What's a mask?"

"A thing like a face."

"Made of stone?" the boy asked quickly.

"No, dear, of paper."

His next inquiries were directed to the Genii who had forgotten all about his promise respecting the gargoyle. "What's a bonfire?" he inquired.

"I'll soon show you what a bonfire is. We'll have one on the night your sister comes—"

"Oh, Ma," cried the delighted boy, running off to his mother with the glad news. "Mr. Dashwood's going to make me a bonfire when sister Sibyl comes."

"Mr. Dashwood spoils you," she replied, pinching his ear.

For Sib was really expected. When Mr. Norman Drummond was thwarted in his attempt to separate her from May, he produced the other Lady Bellmonte's letter (which had been left undated at his request) and propounded a compromise. He had the greatest esteem and regard for Mrs. Bellmonte, and was deeply grieved to find she mistrusted him. He would rejoice exceedingly if reflection should remove her prejudices against him, as he fully believed it would. But his first thoughts must always be for Sib. She required change of air and scene, and it would be so desirable from every point of view if this second ceremony were to take place from her mother's roof; quietly on account of the recent death of her other parent. His father (now a Bishop) would, he felt sure, attend and join their hands. As he spoke he thought of the notice he would put in the *Times*. "*At Garcin Hall, by the Rt. Rev. the*

Lord Bishop of St. Judas, father of the bride-
groom, Norman Drummond, Esquire, barrister-
at-law, to Sibyl, only daughter of the late Sir
George Bellmonte, and sister of the present
baronet." Who could ask unpleasant
questions after *that?* This glorification,
however, he kept to himself, and showed
only the amiable side of his mind. It
would be such a happy opportunity of re-
uniting mother and daughter—so good for
dear Sib. Now if she would go to Garcin
in a week's time, and be married there?

He also repeated in a by-the-by manner
that part of his conversation with the other
Lady Bellmonte of which money matters
were the subject, and enlarged upon the
manly appearance of her son. This made
May waver. Her quick mind took in at

once the immense advantages which would surround a second marriage performed under such auspices (if a second marriage had to be had at all), and into her loving, unselfish heart no shade of envy entered. What if another did take, in some measure, her place in the grand old Hall—that other was Sib.

So the compromise was made, and reported —not as a compromise—to the other Lady Bellmonte, who being now on excellent terms with Drummond on account of his happy selection of a tutor for her darling, wrote quite an affectionate letter to Sib—direct— pressing her to accept the very thoughtful arrangements made by dear Mr. Drummond. She actually called him " dear Mr. Drummond," and had half a mind to write " dear Norman."

The one soft spot in her nature held her boy, and he had improved so wonderfully, thanks to dear Mr. Drummond.

Dashwood kept his word. The night of Sib's arrival there was a grand bonfire right in front of the Hall—and more. He got rockets, and blue fires, and catherine wheels; and Sir George, muffled up in a juvenile ulster, and duly protected with overshoes and comforters, touched them off with his own hands, and lit the pile of tar-barrels himself. How he screamed with delight as the flames shot up !

" If Guy Fawkes were in that," he whispered to his tutor, pointing to the raging fire, " there would be nothing left of him— nothing ! "

When Dashwood said, " Come, the best of it is over, you can see it die out from the windows," he allowed himself to be led back to the house without a murmur.

" Sister Sib," he observed, when he entered the drawing-room, " *that* bonfire was for you."

" You darling ! " cried his mother, seizing him in her arms and kissing him. " What a man he will be, Sibyl ! Thank you so much, Mr. Dashwood, for taking all this trouble. Have you thanked Mr. Dashwood, darling ? "

" Don't thank me," laughed the judicious one; " I enjoyed it quite as much as he did."

" And I know how to make a bonfire myself, now," said the dear child with a sagacious nod of his head.

" *So* quick and clever!" remarked his mother.

The bonfire had a fascination for him very similar to that which the river had once exercised. He watched it from the windows till it was time to go to bed, and often during the night he got up to have another look at the dying embers.

" Ma," said he, ruthlessly rousing his sleeping mother, by the side of whose bed his own was drawn close—for Lady Bellmonte could not rest unless her darling was near—" Ma, the bonfire isn't out yet."

Now if there be a selfish spot in our dispositions, it will show itself when we are sleepy. " Nature's soft nurse " teaches wholesome truths, and I strongly suspect that a good many mothers who declare themselves willing to sacrifice anything for their beloved children would draw the line at being awakened out of a sound sleep, and roughly shaken by cold hands. Even Lady Bellmonte was not proof against this ordeal.

"You shall not get out of bed, you naughty boy! You will take a chill. Go back again directly.

" I wonder if *it* saw the bonfire," he asked, regardless of her injunction.

" ' It !' what ' it ? ' "

" The thing in the library."

" What nonsense! how can a stone see ? "

" It's got eyes."

" Get into bed, you foolish child, you shall not have another bonfire if you get so excited about it."

Lady Bellmonte was not the only dweller in the Hall who had a bad night's rest. Mr. Dashwood went up to his room, cold and sulky.

"That confounded tar-smoke has half-choked me," he muttered, "and my boots are soaked through. What an idiot I am to stand on my head in this way for that little beast. Boo—oo—I have got quite a chill! I will—yes, just for once—I really require it."

So saying he unlocked a drawer, took out a bottle of brandy, poked up the fire, and threw some coals on it.

Next morning at breakfast, Mr. Dashwood sent his compliments and begged to be excused, as he was not feeling well.

"Oh! I'm so sorry," exclaimed Lady
Bellmonte; "I suppose he caught cold at
the bonfire. Do run up, Georgy, like a
good boy, and see if he will not have something—perhaps he'd like a cup of tea. Tell
him to order anything he likes."

Georgy ran up and returned with the
report that Mr. Dashwood didn't want anything or anybody; and was very cross.

"I thought of taking you out to pay a
few calls to-day, Sibyl," said her mother,
when they rose. "It is well that you should
know the people, and have your marriage
formally announced in the neighbourhood."

Sib winced. It was part of the other
Lady Bellmonte's tactics to treat her as
though she were a *fiancée*, even between
themselves—and it hurt a little to be shown

about as Mr. Drummond's *future* wife. But this gauntlet had to be run, and the faster she ran the fewer slaps she was likely to receive. It was well to get it over, so she assented, and noon found them dressed and the carriage at the door.

"Where's Georgy?" asked my lady. "He is coming too."

After some search Georgy was found, but in anything but visiting form. Tar on his hands, tar on his jacket, tar on his nose where he had rubbed it, his pocket-handkerchief being black with the prevailing pigment.

"You naughty boy! what have you been doing?"

"Helping Tom with the yard fence."

"Oh, dear! how often have I told you

not to play with the workmen. This comes of Mr. Dashwood being ill. It really is most inconvenient." Lady Bellmonte spoke as though a tutor had no business with any of the ills that flesh is heir to—except an heir.

" He cannot possibly come with us in this plight," she continued. "And the days are so short, we cannot wait."

" I don't want to go visiting. I hate visiting," said her son, sulkily. " Besides," — brightening up as the thought struck him—" I want to be with poor, dear Mr. Dashwood."

" You see what a heart he has," his mother remarked to Sib, as the carriage was driven off; " and, really, his naughtiness is of a manly sort. I'd sooner he spoiled fifty suits than grow up a milksop."

They paid their visits—and whom they saw, what surprises they gave, and what sort of congratulations they received, matters not here. It was dark when the carriage rolled through the park-gates, and Sib, who was sitting on the side which commanded a view of the Hall, remarked how bright it looked.

"It's the library," replied my lady; "Mr. Moule is there, I suppose; but he really takes too much of a liberty, lighting up the large chandeliers."

"I don't think it is the chandelier," Sib whispered hurriedly. It looks like—"

The word that was on her lips came in a shout from the Hall.

"FIRE!"

The coachman lashed his horses and they

came to the portico in a gallop, but not
before the terror-striking word had been
repeated by a dozen half-frantic domestics;
and the loud alarm-bell was clanging.

The great library was on fire. At the
first suspicion of danger, when the door was
opened, a cloud of black, blinding smoke
dashed into the faces of the seekers, and
drove them back into the vestibule. As Sib
and her mother ran in the house was full
of it; and still it poured forth from the
unclosed door—black, hot, acrid, as no smoke
of mere burning wood should be.

"Georgy! where is Georgy?" shrieked
his mother.

"Shut the doors!" cried Sib—the only
one who had her wits about her — "the
draught only gives it air."

But at this moment a crash, and a sharp tingling, as though of breaking glass, was heard. One of the windows had been reached by the flames, and given way. Then the blinding, choking smoke sought that freer egress to the open air, and the thorough draught brightened up the fire so that Sib, in the act of carrying out her own order, saw clearly into the room.

In the very centre of the library raged a blaze which might have been taken for the bonfire of the night before at its bravest.

The distracted mother, heeding not fire or smoke, rushed from room to room shrieking, " Georgy ! Georgy !" The priceless library might burn—the house might burn— the whole broad lands of Garcin might be

III.   56

strewn with ashes, so that her darling were safe. Where was he?—who had seen him? Ah! dear boy; he was with Mr. Dashwood in the wing, far from danger. To the tutor's room she hurried, so excited, so full of one thought that all minor considerations were forgotten. Without a call, without a knock, in she dashed!—and there on the floor was the judicious Mr. Dashwood, half dressed, and dead drunk; with an empty brandy-bottle in one hand, and three others scattered around him! But no Georgy.

As the flames brightened, and the smoke cleared towards the window, Sib took one step forward into the blazing room. What could be burning like that—right in the middle?—firing the roof above, and dropping red-hot embers on the scorching floor.

Amidst the fiery tongues which darted hissing and crackling up she thought she caught dim outlines of furniture—chairs, tables, the rollers of maps, the covers of books. Oh, impossible!—who could have piled them up so? And on the oaken floor ran a black stream, followed by a lambent flame! What could that be? Tar? Tar in the library of Garcin Hall! Tar! Before the word could form itself on her tongue the thought struck her. Where she stood the heat was scarcely bearable; but uttering a low cry, half-sob, half-wail, she dived (as it were) under the smoke, and made for the very foot of the burning pile.

What was this which Lady Bellmonte— now too frantic even to articulate her cry

of " Georgy ! Georgy !"—saw crawling towards the open door ? The fire ? Yes—the
fire.   But it did not advance alone with its
own deadly march.   Slowly it came along,
and it seemed as though one bundle of
flame were pushing another bundle of flame
before it.

The first was all that was left of Sir
George Bellmonte, and the other his faithful
sister, Sib.

CHAPTER XI.

MR. DRUMMOND IS KNOWN.

"GONE to Garcin to be married!" said Tom Tyrell, who in a temporary access of affection for May, had visited his niece at her lodgings. "That's queer. Does the old lady know all about it?"

He was told that she did, and was behaving, as May added, unexpectedly well.

"What a d— rascal he is!" Tom observed, with one of his foxiest grins. "He knows what he is about."

Mr. Drummond's name had not yet been mentioned, but May knew who the rascal thus past-participled was.

"I don't like him," she said; "I can't like him. Arthur thinks him sincere, and so does dear Lady Bell, and I—I suppose I'm prejudiced and unreasonable ; but I cannot, and I *will* not, believe in him after all."

"All what ?"

"Well, after all his explanations. Who was the wretch who said that a woman's instincts are generally right,—and her reasoning invariably wrong ? "

"Give it up," Tom answered. "Ask me something easier."

"He wrote her a letter that night," May resumed, "begging her pardon, and giving in to what she wanted, before he knew her brother could turn us out. That is what I can't get over, when I reason."

" Are you as fond of Sib as ever ? "

" The darling ! Of course I am."

" Don't you see it hurts your chances like the deuce for her and Drummond to make up ? "

" I don't care a straw for that, uncle. I would rejoice with all my heart for Sib to marry a good man, and have a dozen boys to keep us out of Garcin for ever. I don't care for Garcin now. All I want is to see Sib happy."

" But I want to see you my lady again. *I* do. May, there's foul play going on at Garcin. A fellow has gone down there as tutor to that rickety brat, on Drummond's recommendation. I know him. A drunken scamp who was in my pay once—making radical speeches amongst soldiers, and he was an officer once! There's nothing he would stick at. Suppose this precious Mr. Norman Drummond is trying to get the boy out of the way so that Sib should bring him the estate, eh?"

"Oh no! he's not so bad as that."

"He's bad to the core."

"No. He loves Sib. We can't get over that letter."

"Would you like to see it?"

The expression of the great Reynard himself is open and candid in comparison with that which filled Tom Tyrell's face at that moment.

"Why, you burned it," said May.

"Look here. If a man came to you and blustered about a letter of his to his wife which you had, and threatened all sorts of things if you didn't give it up — and according to his own showing, it was one which would do him good for her to get— and he went away and didn't carry out his threats—and came back again and offered you money for it — what would you do ?"

"Send him away with a flea in his ear."

"And lose two hundred pounds ! That's not the sort of instinct your clever chap meant. You've got to reason about a thing like that."

"Uncle, you've got that letter ?"

"Of course I have."

"Well, it only makes his case clear," May remarked with a sigh. "Let me see it, and then I shall be fully satisfied."

"I knew he'd come back" Tom proceeded, "and so I prepared for him. I opened the envelope over hot water, and read the letter. Even then I thought there was only a row he wanted to make up; but when I heard about the Cowpers, and he offered me two hundred pounds for it, I I knew where I was. That letter was worth more than two hundred pounds to me then. He thought I tore it up and burned it. Lord, what a fool I made of him! There was only a blank sheet inside. What he really wrote is here."

He opened his pocket-book with much deliberation, and spread upon the table what

Mr. Norman Drummond had written the night before Messrs. Boyle and Clerk delivered the brief in *re* Bellmonte.

" *Dear Sib,*

  " *We made a mistake about McPhale's house. It is on the English side of the road. This need make no difference if you will only take a reasonable view of things, and let them stay as they are.*

    " *Yours,*

      " *Norman.*"

This was his way of begging pardon for having treated the subject more lightly than it deserved! This his consent to her request that his father should be invited to the house, and she be presented to him as

his son's wife! This curt and brutal con·
firmation of her worst fears! This proposition to be "*reasonable*," and remain
with him as his mistress !

"The villain!" said May. She did not
feel surprised. She did not pay him the
compliment of starting or screaming at this
revelation. It seemed so natural. What
she could not understand was, how she ever
allowed herself to take his version of this
letter as the correct one, and so make it the
touchstone of his mind.

"So you see," her uncle proceeded, "we
can put a spoke in his little wheel whenever
we feel inclined. I don't take much stock in
Sib, and I oughtn't to lay awake at nights
thinking what I can do for you after the
way you treated me."

"Uncle, the money was not really mine to give. I knew that trouble was hanging over us. I did not know how soon it might fall. If I had been really mistress of Garcin, you should not have asked in vain for ten times the sum."

"Well, well, well; let that be. I forgive you. You make as big a fool of me as I made of Drummond. I ought to have kept all this to myself, gone to him and sold him the letter for two thousand this time. That's what I ought to have done, for my own interests." He spoke sadly, as a man who regretted lost opportunities of doing noble acts. He even emits something between a sniff and a whimper which was intended to be a sigh over the sacrifice. "But I'll give it to you, so that you can stop the marriage. You can do more than that with it. You can stop her marrying *any one*," he added with a foxy wink, "by showing that bit of paper."

Hot blood rushed to May's face, and a hot answer to her tongue. What she had to say in reply to this amiable proposition was checked by the sudden appearance of Arthur.

"May, dearest!" he said quickly, "I've bad news— bad news from Garcin."

"Sib!" she cried.

"There has been a fire. Half the hall is in ruins, Moule telegraphs me. And that poor little boy is dead."

"But Sib! what of Sib, my Sib?"

"Badly burned," he said, "trying to save him. She dragged his body out

of the worst of the fire. She acted
nobly."

"Of course she did — my dear, brave
Sib!" But you are not deceiving me. Is
—is badly burned the worst?"

"The worst I know, dear," Arthur replied
gravely. "I must now go to Drummond,
and——"

"Drummond!" she echoed him. "Good
God, Arthur, I haven't told you. The boy
dead—and Sib! Oh read this, read this
(thrusting Drummond's letter before him),
and tell me what on earth we are to do!
Sib has the estate now. She loves the
wretch, and he will do anything to gain his
point. Our hands are tied. We cannot use
this now; he'll swear it's a forgery if we do,
and she'll believe him."

Even Tom Tyrell was taken aback at this possibility. He reflected upon what might be expected from him under the circumstances.

" We must think it over carefully," said Arthur. " There is plenty of time. The marriage will have to be post-poned."

" I'm not so sure of that," May replied; "remember it was to have been quiet, and private, and by special license. He'll try to hasten it instead, on the ex-cuse that he is wanted at the Hall. Just think! Aunt, frantic with grief; Sib suffering; half the house in ruins. They must have some one to — Arthur, let us put our pride in our pocket and go ourselves."

Mr. Norman Drummond was actually at Garcin—summoned by Sib—before " poor old Moule's" slower mind thought of sending that message to Arthur.   He found more than half the hall in ruins; its unhappy master dead ; Lady Bellmonte in a most pre-carious state ; and Sib with her right arm badly burnt up to the shoulder.   Fortunately, she had not thrown off the thick woollen wraps she wore during her drive, when she rushed into the flames ; and although the burning tar on the floor had set her drapery alight as she crawled in and out, the fire had not penetrated to her person, except as already mentioned.

May was not wrong in divining what Drummond's tactics would be.   Their mar-riage, by special license, was fixed for the

III.   57

following Monday, and the fire in which her brother lost his life had occurred on the Friday night. But there was no room for hurrying on arrangements. To keep to them as they were was all Mr. Drummond wished, but this Sib would not hear of. They could not possibly be carried out before the funeral, she said; and even then she had much to do before she could think about herself.

"You mean about rebuilding the house?" he ventured. "Well, it will not take us long to select a plan, and we can go abroad or to London whilst it is executed."

"That will be for other and cleverer heads than mine, dear," she replied. "It is right that I should tell you at once that I intend to carry out my father's will."

"Will!" he exclaimed with a start; "he left no will."

"On paper—no; but I have learned what his wishes were, and I shall respect them. My poor mother has said things in her delirium, and Mr. Moule has told me others, which show me that my father did not wish that Arthur should be disturbed. My mother, out of love for that unfortunate child, disregarded his desire, and see what has happened."

This took away Mr. Drummond's breath.

"Have you lost your senses?" he gasped.

"Dearest love," she answered him, stretching her sound hand over the table at which they sat, and taking his. "It is right. You will say so yourself when you know what has passed."

Then she told him all she had gleaned from the honest little antiquary; how her father had resolved to destroy the proofs of his legitimacy; how he had sent for him (Moule) in his death-agony, obviously with the intention of giving them to him for suppression; how her mother had become possessed of the papers — and the result. How she had removed the last of the Sinking Stones to—as she thought—a place in which the old prophecy could be defied; how the wretched boy, now lying dead, had been fascinated by the gargoyle, and had tried to destroy it; and how, the floor being burned through, the stone had actually fallen, and (cracked into four fragments by the heat) had sunk into the foundations below the level of the ground! And to all this he repeated, like a man in a dream, "Have you lost your senses?"

His conduct was disappointing. He had told her over and over again that his present income was sufficient for all their wants, and was increasing; had scorned, over and over again, the insinuation that he was moved by her prospects—once so remote—to change his feelings towards her; had assured her, over and over again, that her love was all he sought; and to fulfil her wishes the main object of his life. And now, when he might have thrown his arms around her and said, "Have it as you will, my darling; now I can *prove* my sincerity;"

he sat frowning, and rejected the hand she
proffered !

"As soon as the funeral is over," she
continued, "I shall see Mr. Ucross, and
have the necessary law arrangements made
for putting Arthur and May into possession."

"Not with my consent," he cried, starting
up. "Good Heavens! was anything ever
so absurd, so mad! Think of the position,
think of the influence!"

"You have told me," she replied, "that
you could win for me a higher position; and
as for the influence—Arthur's influence will
be as much at your service as though it
were mine."

"Pshaw!" he scoffed; "you are doing
this to try me."

"Does it try you, Norman?" she asked, looking him full in the face, with her steadfast, tender eyes. "I dare say it does —for the moment. The sacrifice of what we do not expect is easily offered—no, that is unjust, I did not mean that. You are thinking of me. Believe me, dearest, when I say I shall not only do this without regret, but I shall be happy and proud—*so* proud, when by one act of justice I carry out my dear father's wish, and vindicate you."

"You never think of your mother," he answered hotly. "You believe what an old fool says about the intentions of a drunken reprobate, and you outrage your other parent who has been all goodness to you."

"My poor mother!" Sib mused, half

aloud. "How gladly she would undo her acts. There is a curse upon them!"

"Oh, this is sheer lunacy!" he exclaimed. "I decline to discuss the subject with you, Sibyl, until you can approach it in a more reasonable manner."

"Good night," she said sadly; "I must go to my mother now. Won't you kiss me, Norman?"

"There, then, there!" he did not look at the face he just touched with his lips, and returned sulkily to his seat; the Norman of Chelsea who was tired of her.

"If I could only put her into a lunatic asylum!" he muttered to himself. "Her mother could, but she's breaking her heart for that wretched brat, and will not see me. What infernal luck!"

Then he went up to Mr. Dashwood's room, to verify what Sib had said about the " wretched brat," and to send that gentleman about his business; for from the first moment of his arrival he had assumed the airs of master at the Hall, and his late passage of arms with Sib had but slightly chilled them. She was nervous and excited now. She would think better of it when she was more calm, and he had reasoned her superstitions away. Anyhow, he could *seem* to agree with her; get her to put off the execution of her plans until after their marriage; and then — he chuckled at the thought.

From Dashwood, whom he found in a terrible state of depression, caused partly by his drunken bout, and partly (let him have

what credit is due) by remorse, he gained
no materials for reasoning Sib out of her
superstitions ; but, on the contrary, plenty
to confirm them. The unlucky hint about
burning the gargoyle on Guy Fawkes' day
had struck root in the poor boy's simple
mind, and it was only too clear now what
was in it when he told his sister so markedly
that the bonfire was for *her*, but he knew
how to make one for himself. He had not
helped Tom with the stable-fence. He had
watched his opportunity, when Tom's back
was turned, to make off with two buckets
full of tar, which he carried to the almost
unused library, where—imitating what had
been done the day before by his tutor's
orders—he piled around the gargoyle all
the dry material he could move, poured the

tar over the pile, and having torn out the leaves of many priceless volumes to serve in lieu of straw, fired it—reckless, or perhaps ignorant, of the consequences. Whether he had been smothered by the smoke, or had fallen in a fit, will never be known.

On Sunday, Sib received a note, saying that Arthur and May were at the *Bellmonte Arms* in Town Garcin, and would she see them? She sent a carriage instantly, with a peremptory demand that they should come at once to the Hall—" or what is left of it," she said; " but there is plenty of room, and oh! such a welcome! for you." This was a terrible blow to Mr. Drummond, and was made still more severe when he heard that the other Lady Bellmonte (who had refused to see him) had expressed a wish to speak with Arthur.

This story is nearly at its end, and Mr. Norman Drummond's game is quite played out. After three cajoling, and one stormy, conversation with Sib, he found that she was not to be moved from her determination. She would execute her dead father's wish whilst she was a free woman. She was obliged to him for his proffer of assistance, but wanted to do it all herself; and without loss of time she would restore her darling cousins to their rights. She would hold the man who professed to love her to the representations by which he had regained her confidence. And what could he say? Nothing! for his own interests. He had

stopped up every earth against himself in
that quarter, and all he urged in favour of
hers, she easily disposed of.   He had to
back out, and you may be sure his excuses
were plausible, and couched in the very best
language.   He found that Arthur—(again
Sir Arthur, this time permanently so)—and
his wife exercised an influence over Miss
Bellmonte (Mr. Drummond called her so at
last), against which it was hopeless for him
to   struggle — an   influence   which   would
undermine   the   confidence   which   should
exist between husband and wife, and render
them both unhappy.   It was not the loss of
Garcin—oh dear no!—*that* he could have
endured; but the greater sacrifice he was
called upon to make—the loss of Miss Bellmonte's regard evinced by her cleaving to

those whom he could not but regard as his enemies—*that* cut him to the heart, and forced upon him the agonizing conviction that they must part. " Better," he said, with tears in his voice, " it will be for us both to bear this misery, sharp and sudden as it is, than to live long years of estrange-ment and distrust. You have made your choice, and I pray heaven it may be a happy one for you. The time will come," he told her with a well-arranged sob, " when you will know me better."

And he was quite right. It did come. When poor faithful Sib (who half believed in him up to this point, but was too firm in her resolve to give way), fell weeping upon May's neck, and told her of what she thought was only a lover's quarrel to be soon set right in the usual way—that lady produced the letter of which we wot, and Mr. Drummond was known.

"I would never have shown it to you, dear," she said, "if I had any hopes of him. You might have thought—"

"May!"

"You might have thought we were plotting for our own ends, and let me tell you here and now—no! listen.   If you get those deeds made out there'll be another fire into which they go—*they shall!* You are mistress of Garcin, and mistress of Garcin you shall remain till you give it a master; and if I were a fairy godmother I'd get you the best, and the handsomest, and the richest, and the nicest prince in all the world; and I'd give you—

oh Sib, my darling! what can I give you more than my unalterable love."

The other Lady Bellmonte, who could not bear the sight of anything which reminded her of her lost boy, had gone abroad to live upon her dowry, and the *ménage* at the rebuilt Hall was a peculiar, but a very united and happy one. There was a Mrs. Bellmonte, who used to be "my lady," and lived there as *châtelaine;* a Lady Bellmonte, evidently the wife of a gentleman who called himself the Land Steward when out of hearing of a lady who was once known as Miss Cowper, then as Mrs. Drummond, and was now (as heiress-at-law of Sir George Bellmonte, deceased), the untitled lady of Garcin. And there was at the time I write (five years after the fire) a person (aged four) who was monarch of all he surveyed, and was the darling of them all—especially of Cousin Sib.   He answered to the name of Arty, and if he grew up to be a man would be Sir Arthur Bellmonte of Garcin.   And he had a little sister called Sibyl.

Mr.   Norman   Drummond   prospered. Juniors in the back rows call the leaders of their circuits and the Chief Justices by their surnames *tout court*, but he was always *Mr.* Drummond.   He wore black kid gloves in Court, and visited Duchesses.   He was wise enough to hold his peace on a certain subject, and though the great world thought Miss Bellmonte was "a woman with a history," on account of her many refusals to change her state, it could not say exactly what that history was.   When she read one day in

III.   58

a fashionable weekly that a marriage was arranged between Mr. Drummond, Q.C. and the Lady Louisa Bankside, second daughter of the Earl and Countess of Pentonville, old memories gave a clutch at her heart, and for a moment quickened its pulsations. Only for a moment. She took little Arthur on her lap, and kissed him.

Tom Tyrell has not got into Parliament yet; which was a pity, for he did a good deal more mischief out of it, where he was not answered, than he could possibly do in that august assembly.

The fatal gargoyle, cleft into four, remained where it fell in the foundations of Garcin Hall. Does this mean that only four generations of Bellmontes are to flourish? I am getting on in years, and as

I cannot hope to see May a grandmother, I really must give it up.

Old Moule said it was all right—so I suppose it is.

THE END.

BUNGAY : CLAY AND TAYLOR, PRINTERS.'   S. & H.